SUSAN MALLERY

A Fool's Gold Christmas

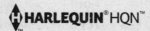

HARLEQUIN® HQN™

Recycling programs
for this product may
not exist in your area.

ISBN-13: 978-0-373-77788-4

A FOOL'S GOLD CHRISTMAS

Copyright © 2012 by Susan Macias Redmond

Printed in U.S.A.

Dear Reader,

'Tis the season in Fool's Gold, a time of sparkly lights, warm holiday greetings and, of course, romance. Although reading may seem like a solitary activity, we romance readers are as much a community as the small town of Fool's Gold. Our first reaction when reading a great love story is to tell a friend about it. We want to share that happy feeling.

I've been blessed with the most enthusiastic readers a writer could ever hope for. Last year, I invited my fans to try out for the Fool's Gold Varsity Cheerleading Squad, to earn prizes simply for telling people about Fool's Gold and the books they love. The women selected for the team took my breath away. They drove to their local bookstores with Fool's Gold car magnets, wearing Fool's Gold T-shirts, hats and pins, and handed out bookmarks, placed the books in readers' hands and said, "You will love this!" Yes, they won lots of prizes along the way—including the dedication in this book—but I could never thank them enough for their generosity.

This book is for those of you who love romance, love to read and then tell your friends about the latest, greatest book you just finished. It is also for my wonderful cheerleaders.

If being a Fool's Gold Varsity Cheerleader sounds like fun to you, be sure to join the Members Only area at www.susanmallery.com so I can email you the next time we hold cheerleader tryouts.

In the meantime, from my heart to yours, Merry Christmas! May all your dreams come true.

Susan

To the 2011 Head Cheerleader, Char,
who has such an amazing heart that she
wanted to share this dedication with the entire
Fool's Gold Varsity Cheerleading squad in the
spirit of Christmas. This one is for you.

A Fool's Gold Christmas

One

THE SOUND OF eight tiny reindeer had nothing on a half-dozen eight-year-olds clog dancing, Dante Jefferson thought as he held the phone more closely to his ear.

"You'll have to repeat that," he yelled in to the receiver. "I'm having trouble hearing you."

The steady thudding above his head paused briefly, then started up again.

"What's going on there?" Franklin asked, his voice barely audible over the banging that nearly kept time with the damned piano music. "Construction?"

"I wish," Dante muttered. "Look, I'll call you back in a couple of hours." The stupid dance class would be over by then. At least he hoped so.

"Sure. I'll be here." Franklin hung up.

Dante glanced at the bottom right of his computer screen. The ever-present clock told him it was seven-fifteen. In the evening. Which meant it was eleven-fifteen in the morning in Shanghai. He'd stayed late specifically to speak to Franklin about an international business deal that had developed a few glitches. The clog dancers had made the conversation impossible.

He saved the spreadsheet and went to work on his email. He and his business partner had plenty of other projects that needed his attention.

Just before eight, he heard the clog dancers going down the stairs. They laughed and shrieked, obviously not worn out by an hour of misstepping practice. He, on the other hand, had a pounding pain right behind his eyes and the thought that he would cheerfully strangle Rafe first thing in the morning. His business partner had been the one to rent the temporary space. Either Rafe hadn't noticed or didn't care about the dance school parked directly above. The offices were in an older part of Fool's Gold and had been built long before the invention of soundproofing. Rafe didn't seem to mind the noise that started promptly at three every single afternoon and went well into the evening. Dante, on the other hand, was ready to beg the nearest judge for an injunction.

Now he got out of his chair and headed for the stairs. He made his way to the studio. He and whoever was in charge were going to have to come to terms. He had to spend the next couple of weeks working out the problems of the Shanghai deal.

Which meant needing access to his computer, contracts and blueprints. Some of which he couldn't take home. He needed to able to use his phone, in his *office,* while speaking in a normal voice.

He paused outside the door that led to the studio. It was as old-fashioned as the rest of the building, with frosted glass and the name of the business—Dominique's School of Dance—painted in fancy gold script. He pushed open the door and entered.

The reception area was utilitarian at best. There was a low desk, a computer that had been old a decade ago, backless benches by the wall and several coatracks. He could see through into the studio itself—a square room with mirrors, a barre that was attached to the wall and, of course, hardwood floors. There wasn't a piano, and he realized the endless, repetitive song that had driven him insane had come from a compact stereo.

He rubbed his temples and wished the pounding would stop, then walked purposefully into the studio. He was a coldhearted bastard lawyer, or so he'd been told endlessly by those he bested. He planned to reduce the dance instructor to a blob of fear, get her to agree to lay off with the dancing and then go back to his phone call. All in the next ten minutes.

"We have to talk," he announced as he came to a halt in the center of the room.

He realized there were mirrors on three walls, so he was seeing himself from unfamiliar angles. His shirt was wrinkled, his hair mussed, and he looked tired, he thought briefly, before turning his attention to—

Dante swore under his breath as he took in the tall, slender woman dressed in nothing more than a black leotard and tights. Despite the fact that she was covered from collarbone to toes, the clinging outfit left nothing to the imagination. He almost felt as if he'd walked in on a woman undressing. A sexy woman with big green eyes and honey-blond hair. A woman who was completely untouchable, for a host of reasons.

He ground his teeth together. Why hadn't Rafe mentioned that his sister was now working here? But even if his business partner didn't kill him for looking, Dante had a firm list of rules that were never broken. Not getting emotionally involved was number one. Anyone who taught little kids to dance had to be softhearted. Nothing got him running faster than a hint of emotion.

"What are you doing here?" Evangeline Stryker asked.

Yes, he thought as he stared at her. Rafe's baby sister. She was responsible for the nightmare that was his life. She and those unbelievably loud mini-dancers she taught. So much for reducing the dance instructor to anything.

"Dante?"

"Sorry," he said, doing his best to keep his voice from growling. "I didn't know you worked here."

Evie gave him a wide-eyed stare, then a strange half laugh. "Right. I work here. I teach dance. Lucky me."

Dante knew Evie had broken her leg a few months ago, but he didn't remember hearing anything about a head injury. "Are you all right?"

"No," she snapped and put her hands on her hips. "Do I look all right?"

He took a step back, not wanting to get in the middle of whatever she had going on. "I came upstairs because I can't work like this anymore. The pounding, the same piece of music playing over and over again. I have to talk to Shanghai tonight, and instead of peace and quiet, there were clog dancers. You've got to make it stop."

He held out both hands, palms up, speaking in what he knew to be his most reasonable tone.

"Make it stop? Make it *stop?*" Her voice rose with each word. "Are you kidding?"

EVIE KNEW SHE sounded shrill. She was sure she was wide-eyed, flushed and more than a little scary, but right now she didn't care. She was in full panic mode and now Dante was stuck listening to her rant.

"You want to talk to me about your troubles?"

she continued. "Fine. Here are mine. In approximately six weeks it's Christmas Eve. That night, the town of Fool's Gold expects yet another chance to see their annual favorite—*The Dance of the Winter King*. You've never heard of it, you say? I know. Me, either. But it's a huge deal here. Huge!"

She paused for breath, wondering if it was possible for her head to actually explode. She could feel a sort of panicked pressure building. It was as if she was in a nightmare where she was going to be naked in front of a room full of strangers. Not that being naked in front of a room full of people she knew was any better.

"I won't go into the details about the storyline," she continued, her chest getting tighter and tighter. "Let's just say it's a lot of students dancing. Oh, and the dances they're doing this year are different than the ones they did last year because, hey, they move up. Which wouldn't be a problem because there's always Miss Monica, who's been teaching here for the last five-hundred-and-fifty years."

She was getting shrill again, she realized, and consciously lowered her voice. "The only problem is Miss Monica has run off with her gentleman friend. The woman has to be pushing seventy, so I should probably be impressed or at least respectful that she has a love life, except she took off with no warning. She left me a note."

Evie pointed to the piece of paper still taped to the mirror.

"She's gone," she repeated. "Left town. Flying out of the country first thing in the morning. Which leaves me with close to sixty girls to teach dances I don't know for a production I've never heard of, let alone seen. There's no choreography to speak of, I'm not sure of the music and I heard the sets are old and need to be completely refurbished. In the next six weeks."

She paused for air. "It's up to me. Do you want to know how long I've been teaching dance? Two months. That's right. This is my first ever, on the planet, teaching job. I have sixty girls depending on me to make their dreams come true. Their dreams of being beautiful and graceful, because you know what? For some of them, this is all they have."

She knew she was skating uncomfortably close to talking about herself. About how, when she'd been younger, dance had been all *she'd* had. She might not have any teaching experience, but she knew what it was like to want to be special and, by God, she was going to make that happen for her students.

She stalked toward him and jabbed her finger into his chest. More specifically, she felt the cool silk of his fancy tie. It probably cost more than she spent on groceries in a month. She didn't

know very much about Dante Jefferson beyond
the fact that he was her brother's business partner and therefore disgustingly rich. Okay—he was
reasonably good-looking, but that didn't help her
right now, so she wasn't going to care.

"If you for one second think I'm going to stop
having practice here," she told him, "you can forget it. I have a serious crisis. If you want to have a
conversation with Shanghai, you can do it somewhere else. I'm hanging on by a thread and when
it snaps, we're all going down."

Dante stared at her for a long moment, then
nodded. "Fair enough."

With that, he turned and walked out of the studio.

She glared at his retreating back. Sure. *He* got
to leave and go back to his fancy life. Not her.
She had to figure out what to do next. While running in circles and screaming might feel good in
the moment, it wasn't going to get the job done.
Nor was railing at the unfairness, kicking something or eating chocolate. She might have failed
in other areas of her life, but she wasn't going to
fail her students.

"You have to rally," she told herself. "You're
tough. You can do it."

And she would, she thought as she sank onto
the floor and rested her head on her knees. She
would figure out *The Dance of the Winter King*

and teach her students and let them have one magical night.

First thing in the morning. But now, she was going to take a few minutes and feel massively sorry for herself. It was a small thing to ask, and she'd earned it.

THE NEXT MORNING, Evie started her day with a heart full of determination. She had survived worse than this before and probably would have to again. Mounting a production she'd never seen with no help might seem daunting, but so what? Her pep talk lasted through her first cup of coffee, then faded completely, leaving the sense of panic to return and knot her stomach. Obviously the first step was to stop trying to do this all alone. She needed help. The question was, where to get it.

She was new in town, which meant no support network. Well, that wasn't totally true. Her brothers had taken a surprising interest in her lately. Rafe had even prepaid for her townhouse, against her wishes. But they would be useless in this situation, her mother wasn't an option and going up to strangers to ask them what they knew about *The Dance of the Winter King* seemed questionable at best. Which left the women in her brothers' lives.

She had one sister-in-law and two sisters-in-law to-be. Of the three of them, Charlie seemed the easiest to approach. She was blunt but kind-hearted. So after a quick routine of stretching to overcome the stiffness of her still-healing leg, Evie got dressed and started out for the center of town.

Fool's Gold was a small town nestled in the foothills of the Sierra Nevada—on the California side. The residential areas boasted tidy lawns and well-kept houses while the downtown held nearly a half-dozen traffic lights, making it practically metropolitan. There were plenty of pumpkins by front doors and paper turkeys in windows. Orange, red and yellow leaves flew across the sidewalk. It had yet to snow at this elevation, but the temperatures were close to freezing at night, and the ski resorts higher up the mountain had opened the previous weekend.

The whole place was one happy small town postcard, Evie thought, shoving her hands into her coat pockets and longing to be somewhere else. Los Angeles would be nice. Warm and, hey, big enough that nobody knew her name—which was how she preferred things. She just wanted to live her life without getting involved with other people. Was that too much to ask?

A stupid question, she reminded herself. She was here now, and responsible for a holiday tradition. She would get it right because she knew what it was like to be disappointed, and there was no way she was doing that to her students.

She rounded a corner and walked up to the fire station in the center of town. The building was older, mostly brick, with giant garage doors that would open if there was an emergency.

Charlie was a firefighter. From what Evie had been able to piece together, Charlie drove one of the big trucks. She was competent, sarcastic and just a little intimidating. She was also a bit of a misfit, which made Evie more comfortable around her. In addition, Clay, Evie's youngest brother, was crazy about her. Over-the-moon, can't-stop-looking-at-her in love.

Clay had been married before, and Evie had adored his late wife. Now that she thought about it, Clay kind of had extraordinary taste when it came to women. After years of mourning his first wife, he'd stumbled into a relationship with Charlie, only to find himself giving his heart and everything else he had. It was kind of nice to see someone as perfect as Clay brought to his knees by an emotion.

Evie hesitated by the entrance leading into the fire station. She told herself to just open the door and walk in. Which she would. In a second. It was just…asking for help was not her favorite thing. She could easily list ninety-seven ways she would rather spend her time. Maybe more.

The door swung open unexpectedly, and Charlie Dixon stepped out. "Evie? Are you okay?"

Charlie was a little taller than Evie, and much bigger. The other woman was all broad shoulders and muscle. The latter no doubt necessary because of her job. Evie had spent her life in search of the perfect combination of being strong enough to dance and thin enough to look good in whatever costume her job required. Which meant being hungry every day of her life since her fourteenth birthday.

"Hey, Charlie," Evie said and forced a smile. "Do you have a second?"

"Sure. Come on in."

The fire station was warm and brightly lit. The big trucks gleamed, and holiday music played over a hidden sound system. Charlie led the way to a massive kitchen with seating for maybe fifteen or twenty, long counters and a six-burner, restaurant-style stove. A big pot of coffee sat by the window, and there was an open box of donuts on the table.

Charlie poured them each a mug of coffee and handed her one, then settled right next to the box of donuts and grabbed a maple bar. As Evie watched, she took a bite and chewed.

Just like that, Evie thought, both impressed and horrified. Depending on the size of the donut, the maple bar would be anywhere from two hundred and fifty calories to over five hundred. Evie had learned shortly after puberty, she was destined to be pear-shaped, with every extra ounce going to her hips, thighs and butt. While the medical community might want her to believe that pear-shaped was perfectly healthy, more than one costume director had pointed out no one wanted to watch a ballerina with a big ass and jiggly thighs.

Evie gripped her coffee mug with both hands, averted her gaze from the box of donuts, whose contents had started to quietly call her name, and stared at Charlie.

"I wondered if I could talk to you about *The Dance of the Winter King.* Do you know about the production?"

"Sure," Charlie said, dropping half the donut onto a napkin and reaching for her coffee. "It happens every year on Christmas Eve. It's kind of a big deal." She smiled, her blue eyes bright with humor. "That's right. You're working for Miss Monica now. Nervous about the big show?"

"You have no idea." Evie knew the situation was complicated even more by the fact that, while Miss Monica was in charge of the studio, the business had recently been purchased by Charlie's mother. Evie had left the new owner a message the previous night, bringing her up-to-date, but had yet to hear from her.

"Miss Monica ran off yesterday." Evie quickly explained about the older woman's flight with her gentleman friend. "I've never seen the dance, and there aren't very many notes on the production. Miss Monica mentioned many of the sets need to be refurbished, and I don't even know where they're kept. I have sixty students who expect to dance in front of their families in six weeks and no idea what I'm doing. Worse, there aren't any videos of the production in the studio. If Miss Monica had any, they're in her house, and she's on her way to Italy."

She stopped and forced herself to inhale. The panic had returned and with it the need for sugar. She started to reach for a small, plain cake donut, then gave in to the inevitable and picked up a chocolate glazed. As her teeth sank into the sweet, light center, the world slowly righted itself.

Charlie ran her hands through her short hair and groaned. "I'm trying desperately not to imagine Miss Monica and her gentleman friend."

Evie chewed and swallowed. "I know exactly what you mean. The terror helps me overcome that image."

"I'll bet." Charlie reached for her coffee. "Okay, let me think. I've seen the dance every year I've been in town, but I can't remember the details. So, start with your students. Their parents will have the production on video, right? You can watch them and figure out what's going on."

Evie sagged back in the chair and nodded.

"You're right. They'll all have it filmed. That's perfect. Thanks."

Charlie stood and moved back toward the kitchen. She pulled open a drawer. When she returned to the table, she had a pad of paper and a pen.

"The sets are going to be in one of the warehouses on the edge of town. There should be a receipt for the monthly rent in the studio's records. This is the guy who manages the warehouses." She wrote down a name. "Tell him who you are, and he'll let you in, even without a key. Then you can evaluate the sets. Let me know how much work there is and we'll organize a work party."

Evie blinked at her. "A what?"

"A work party. People come and help repair the sets. You'll have to provide the materials, but they'll give you all the labor you need."

"I don't understand. You mean there's a group I can hire to fix the sets?" She wasn't sure what the budget would be. Maybe her new boss would want to cancel the production completely.

Charlie sighed and patted her hand. "Not hire. People will help you with the sets for free. Because they want to."

"Why?"

"Because this is Fool's Gold and that's what we do. Just pick a day and I'll get the word out. Trust me, it will be fine."

"Sure," Evie murmured, even though she didn't believe it for a second. Why would people she didn't know show up to work on sets for her production? For free? "I don't suppose these miracle workers can also alter costumes and do hair for the show?"

"Probably not, but there are a couple of salons in town." Charlie wrote on the paper again. "Someone's been taking care of all that every year. Start here. Ask them who normally handles the hair and makeup for the show. I suspect it's either Bella or Julia. Maybe both." She picked up the second half of her maple bar. "They're feuding sisters who own competing salons. It makes for some pretty fun entertainment."

Evie's recently injured leg began to ache. "Let me see if I have this straight. I'm going to talk to parents of my students to get videos of a production I've never seen so I can teach it to their daughters. In the meantime, a man who doesn't know me from a rock is going to let me into a warehouse so I can evaluate the sets. You're going to arrange a work party of perfect strangers to repair those sets—all of which will happen for free. Then feuding sister stylists may or may not know who does the hair and makeup for my sixty dancers."

Charlie grinned. "That about sums it up. Now

tell me the truth. Do you feel better or worse than you did before you got here?"

Evie shook her head. "Honestly? I haven't a clue."

Two

EVIE WALKED HOME after her last class that evening. The night was cool and clear and smelled like fall. All leaves and earth and woodsmoke. She might be more a big-city girl, but there were things she liked about Fool's Gold. Not having to drive her car everywhere was nice, as was being able to see stars in the sky. Now if only she could find a good Chinese place that delivered.

She turned onto her street, aware that most of the townhouses had Thanksgiving decorations in the windows and on the porches. She'd only been in her place a few weeks—it was a rental and had come furnished. She wasn't interested in putting down roots, and buying furniture wasn't in her budget. But maybe she should stick a flameless candle in the window or something.

Somewhere a door slammed shut. She heard laughter and a dog barking. Homey sounds. For a second she allowed herself to admit she was, well, lonely. Except for her family, she barely knew any-one in town. The most contact she'd had with her neighbors had been to wave to the young couple who lived across the street. She'd never even seen the people next door.

She couldn't shake the feeling of being out of place. The sensation wasn't new. In Los Angeles, she'd had plenty of friends but no real direction for her life. She'd been waiting for something. A sign. She'd been going through the motions of liv-ing without a sense of belonging. She'd always fig-ured "one day" she would have the answer. Now she was starting to think there wasn't going to be one day. There was now, and it was up to her to figure out what she wanted.

One of those would be a start, she thought with a quiet laugh as a fancy black sedan pulled into the driveway next to hers. Actually she would settle for having over a hundred dollars in her checking account at any given time.

Evie watched the driver's door open and pre-pared to at least pretend to be friendly. But her halfhearted wave had barely begun when she rec-ognized Dante Jefferson.

"What are you doing here?" she asked. Was he checking on her? Typical. Her brothers couldn't even get the address right. Dante was in the wrong driveway.

"I live here."

"Where?"

He pointed to the townhouse next to hers.

She dropped her arm to her side. "Seriously? For how long?"

"I moved in the weekend after you."

"You knew you were moving in next to me?" she asked.

He shrugged. "There weren't a lot of choices. I don't know if I want to buy or not, so I took a short-term lease. Hungry?"

"What?" She was still dealing with the fact that her brother's business partner was her neighbor.

Dante pulled a large white bag out of the car. "I got Italian. There's plenty. Come on." He started toward his front door before she could decide if she was going to say yes or not.

He was her brother's business partner. That alone was reason enough to say no. He was connected with her family, and she wanted to avoid her family. Mostly because every time she was around them, she got hurt. It was a rule she'd learned early—people who were supposed to love you usually didn't. Staying far, far away meant keeping herself safe.

"And wine," he called over his shoulder.

She could have ignored the bag of food and the offer of wine except for two things. Her stomach growled, reminding her she was starving. And a very delicious smell drifted to her.

"Garlic bread?" she asked, inhaling the fragrance of garlic as visions of cheesy goodness made her mouth water.

Dante paused at the front door and laughed. "Sure. Thanks for making it clear your willingness to have dinner with me is about the menu and not my sparkling personality."

"I really shouldn't," she began, even as she took a step toward him.

He smiled and shook the bag again. "Come on. Just this once. You can do it."

Just this once, she agreed silently. That would be safe.

She walked up and joined him on the porch. He handed her the bag containing dinner, then opened the front door and flipped on the light.

His place was the mirror image of hers, with a living-dining area, a small gas fireplace and the kitchen beyond. She knew there was a half-bath tucked under the stairs. The second floor had a master and a second bedroom with an attached full bath.

Dante's furnishings were all black leather and glass. From his place in San Francisco, she would guess, setting the food on the table and shrugging out of her coat. Her brother had mentioned Dante had moved from the coastal city just a few months ago.

Dante dropped his suit jacket and tie onto the

sofa. He rolled up his sleeves to his elbows as he walked into the kitchen. He was tall, she thought, taking in the short blond hair and killer blue eyes. The man was easy on the eyes. Her gaze dropped as he moved to the cupboards. Nice butt. He moved well. Athletic. He'd been a jock once and kept in shape.

"I'm going to use the guest bath," she said, motioning to the short hallway on the right.

"Help yourself."

She ducked inside and quickly washed her hands. Her face was pale, her eyes too large. She looked tired. No doubt because she was still healing.

By the time she returned to the dining area, Dante had opened the wine and poured. There were plates and paper napkins. Several containers of food were open on the bar area.

"Help yourself," he told her.

"A take-out buffet. Very nice." She took lasagna and a bit of salad, along with two slices of garlic bread. Her brain quickly added up the calories, but she dismissed the number. Staying at her dancing weight wasn't an issue anymore. Besides, she was tired of being hungry.

They sat across from each other. She leaned back in her chair, picked up her glass of wine and smiled. "How are things in Shanghai?"

"Better. We're building a high-rise and the permits have come through." He paused. "I'm going to guess you don't want the actual details."

"You can tell me if it's important."

"You'll pretend interest?"

She laughed. "Yes. Even wide-eyed amazement if it's called for."

"I'll take a rain check." He studied her. "How about your crisis? Getting any better? You aren't as..." He hesitated.

"Shrill?" she asked.

"I would have picked a different word."

"A smart man who understands women." She picked up her fork. "I'm still dealing with everything that's happening, but I'll get through it."

"How's the leg?"

Evie winced. Not something she wanted to talk about.

For two years she'd been a cheerleader for the Los Angeles Stallions football team. Earlier this season, she'd been plowed down by one of the players. She'd fractured a bone, torn a few tendons and generally ended any chance she'd had at ever dancing again professionally.

In a belated attempt to take care of her, her family had converged on the hospital. When she'd been released, they'd taken advantage of her still-drugged state and brought her to Fool's Gold. When she'd finally surfaced, she'd discovered her belongings moved, her physical therapy set up and her brothers and mother hovering. She'd gotten a job at the dance studio and moved out as soon as she was able. But in a town this small, it was impossible to escape them completely.

The bright spot in her recent, uncomfortable past was she'd discovered she loved teaching dance. She'd always been the one to help classmates conquer difficult steps and passages. She might not have the necessary brilliance to be a star, but she understood how to break down a dance and teach it to others. Funny how she'd never thought to turn that into a career. But working with her students had her thinking she might finally have found the direction she'd been looking for.

"I'm healing," she said. "There are a few lingering aches and pains, but nothing I can't handle."

He took a bite of lasagna, swallowed and chewed. "Did the manager of the studio really take off and leave you with the Christmas program?"

"*The Dance of the Winter King,* open to all faiths," she corrected and nodded. "She sure did. You'd think life in a place like this would be easy, but it's not. There are expectations and complicated relationships."

"Like?"

She drew in a breath. "Okay, Miss Monica ran the studio and she's the one who hired me. But the owner is Dominique Guérin." She paused.

Dante waited expectantly.

"You've never heard of her?" she asked.

"No. Should I have?"

"She's a famous ballerina. Or she was. You're not into dance or the dance world, are you?"

"Do I look like I'm into dance?"

"Fair enough." Although he had nice bone structure, she thought. "Then let's try this another way. Dominique is Charlie's mother."

Dante stared at her. "Clay's Charlie?"

"Uh-huh."

"But Charlie's..." He took a big bite of lasagna and mumbled something unintelligible.

She grinned. "What was that?" she asked sweetly.

He motioned to his still-full mouth, as if indicating there was no way he could possibly speak.

"I understand the point you're avoiding," she said. "Charlie doesn't look like a dancer. From what I understand, she takes after her father. Anyway, I've left a message for Dominique to tell her what's going on with the dance studio, but I haven't heard back. In the meantime, I have to assume we're still planning on the Christmas Eve performance, which means getting organized in ways I'm not sure I can even comprehend. I've never been in charge like this before."

Her appetite faded, and she pushed away her plate. "Charlie suggested I ask some of the parents for copies of any recordings they have. So

I'll be able to see those. Then there are costumes and steps and music." She stopped. "We should change the subject or I'll get shrill again. Neither of us wants that."

He swallowed. "It's a lot."

She poked at her salad. "Like I said, we can talk about something else." She looked at him. "So, how did you meet my brother?"

"Rafe?"

"He's the one you do business with. I'm assuming you met Shane and Clay through him."

Dante leaned back in his chair. "You don't know?"

"We're not that close." She'd left for Juilliard when she was seventeen and hadn't had a whole lot of contact with her family ever since. She'd seen them more since her football accident than she had in the past eight years.

"Even to your mom?" he asked.

She sighed. "Let me guess. You and your mom are close and you call at least twice a week. For what it's worth, I really admire that." From an emotional distance, she thought. No way she could relate to it.

Dante picked up his wine. "My mother died a long time ago."

"Oh." Evie felt herself flush. "I'm sorry."

"Like I said, it was a long time ago." He leaned

toward her. "Rafe and I met while we were both in college. We were working construction."

She remembered that her brother had taken summer jobs to supplement his scholarships. After finding out about Dante's mother, she wasn't going to do any more assuming.

"You went into the family business?" she asked.

He chuckled. "No, I was paying the bills. I found out I was a lot more popular with girls in college when I could afford to take them on dates. I was a scholarship student, too."

"Intelligent and good-looking," she teased. "So why are you still single?"

"I like the chase, but I'm not so big on the catch."

"A man who avoids commitments." She knew the type. With those broad shoulders and blue eyes, he would have no trouble getting a woman to notice him. The money and success wouldn't hurt, either. "Do they line up at a set time, or is it more like concert lotteries? You pass out numbers and then call them randomly?"

"Impressive," he told her. "Mocking me and my dates at the same time."

"I was gently teasing. There's a difference."

"You're right." He studied her over his wineglass. "What about you? No fancy Mr. King of the Dance coming to rescue you from the backwater that is Fool's Gold?"

"I'm between kings right now. And, at the risk of sounding like Jane Austen, content to be so. Miss Monica is welcome to her gentleman friend. I'm more focused on the upcoming performance." Not to mention avoiding her family as much as possible.

"Did you see all the Thanksgiving decorations around town?" he asked.

"The turkey population is well represented."

"Christmas is going to be worse," he grumbled.

"Candy canes on every mailbox."

"Wreaths on every door." He looked at her. "It's going to be like living in a snow globe."

"Tell me about it." She sipped her wine. "Do you know this town doesn't have a grocery store that stays open twenty-four hours a day? What's up with that? What if someone needs something at two in the morning?"

"Like aspirin after listening to clog dancers for an hour?"

"You'll adore them when you see them perform."

"Maybe." He frowned. "Hey, why aren't you a big fan of Christmas? With your family, I would think loving the season would be a given. I'll bet your mom made Christmas special for you."

Evie put down her wine and pressed a hand to her stomach. Sudden churning made her uncomfortable.

No doubt Dante saw May as a warm, caring parent. The kind of woman who would bake cookies and sew Christmas stockings. Maybe she had once—Evie's brothers each had a carefully embroidered stocking. But Evie's was store-bought and not personalized. There hadn't been many traditions for her. She'd always found Christmas kind of lonely and wasn't looking forward to an entire town showing her all the ways she didn't fit in.

"I suppose I've gotten out of the habit of the holidays," she said, hedging. She barely knew Dante. There was no reason to go into the gory details of her past with the man.

"Then we'll have to stay strong together," he told her. "There's only the two of us against all of them."

She laughed. "Grinches together?"

"Absolutely." He pointed at her nearly untouched plate. "Okay, you're either going to have to eat more or explain to the chef why you didn't like his very excellent lasagna."

"I wouldn't want that."

An hour later, they'd finished most of the wine. Dante had explained more about the Shanghai project and she'd told funny stories about her days touring with a third-rate ballet company. He insisted on packing up the leftovers for her to take home and then escorted her across their shared driveway and to her front door. Once there, he waited until she'd put her key in the lock and pushed open the door.

"If you need anything, pound on the wall," he told her. "Ah, the one between us. If you pound on the other one, you'll confuse the neighbors and get a bad reputation in the development."

"I wouldn't want that." She held up the bag of food. "Thanks for this."

"You're skinny. Eat more." With that, he bent down and lightly kissed her cheek. "'Night, Evie."

"'Night."

She watched him walk back to his place and step inside. Then she stepped into her house and shut the door. She stood in the dark for a second, the feel of his kiss lingering on her cheek.

She'd had fun tonight. Talking, sharing a meal with a friend. Dante was easy to talk to. Charming. He was the kind of man who made a woman think about more than kissing. Even someone who knew how dangerous that could be.

"My brother's business partner and a player," she said as she turned on the light in the entryway. There were a thousand reasons not to play the what-if game with Dante Jefferson. She was smart enough to remember every one of them.

"YOU KNOW THIS isn't normal, right," Dante said as he stood on the porch of the house and stared out at the elephant. "Ranches are supposed to have things like horses and goats. What were you thinking?"

Rafe shook his head. "It wasn't me."

Dante continued to study the elephant. "What is she wearing?"

"A blanket. It gets cold here. She goes into a heated barn at night, but she likes to be out during the day. Mom had the blanket made for her."

Dante thought longingly of his life back in San Francisco. Season tickets to the Giants and the 49ers. Poker nights with his buddies. Dinners with beautiful women. Okay, sure, he'd had a beautiful woman at his place last night, but that was different. She was his partner's sister. The price of getting lucky could be the loss of a very treasured body part. Although he would have to admit watching Evie move was almost worth it. He supposed it was years of dance training, but she made even the act of picking up a fork look graceful.

"I know what you're thinking," Rafe said.

Dante doubted that.

"I changed my life for Heidi," Rafe continued. "It's worth it. And I want to be here on the ranch. I like Fool's Gold."

"I figured as much when you moved the business here."

"Come on." Rafe turned toward the house. "Let's go inside. We'll have brownies while you tell me about what's going on in Shanghai."

They settled at the kitchen table. The company's rented office space didn't have any private offices, which meant any sensitive business had to be discussed elsewhere.

Over the next couple of hours, they reviewed several ongoing projects, and Dante brought Rafe up-to-date on a few legal matters. When they were finished, Rafe poured them each more coffee.

"You staying in Fool's Gold for Thanksgiving?" he asked.

Dante shrugged. "Probably."

"Come to dinner, then. I wasn't going to get between you and your latest conquest, but if you're flying solo, we'd love to have you."

"Thanks. I'll bring wine."

"Not a salad or dessert?" Rafe joked.

"Maybe next year." He collected the folders he'd brought. "Evie's pretty panicked about the Christmas Eve dance show."

Rafe frowned. "What are you talking about?"

"The show. *The Dance of the Winter King.* The manager of the dance studio took off and left everything to her."

"I didn't know that."

The statement confirmed what Evie had hinted at the previous night. That she and her family didn't have much to do with each other.

"You and your brothers have always been close," Dante said. "But you barely mention Evie.

We'd been in business about three years before I even knew you had a sister. What's up with that?"

Rafe shrugged. "After my dad died, things were tough. My mom was devastated, money was tight. I tried to handle the family, but I was a kid."

Eight or nine, Dante thought, remembering what his friend had told him over the years. He knew what it was like to look out for a parent. He'd done the same with his mom. It had always been the two of them against the world. Until Dante had joined a gang. His actions had broken her heart and ultimately cost her everything.

What he would give to go back and change that, he thought grimly. To have his family back. But he'd learned about the perils of close ties.

"Mom was crying all the time," Rafe continued. "We knew she was sad. Shane met this cowboy in town for one of the festivals and brought him home for dinner. Nine months later, Evie showed up."

"You're kidding."

"No. She's technically our half sister. The four of us were a unit and Evie never seemed to find her place. I should have tried harder with her. I'm trying now. I don't know that it's enough." He stared at Dante. "You live close to her, don't you?"

"Next door." Dante braced himself for the next line. Where Rafe said to stay away from his sister.

"So do me a favor. Look out for her. Make sure she's okay."

That was it? No dire warning? Rafe knew Dante's reputation with women. It's not that Dante was a bad guy—he simply didn't believe in long-term commitments. Four months was a personal best in his world.

"Sure thing," he said easily. "I'm happy to help."

"Good. She'd tell me that it's too little, too late, but as far as I'm concerned, having Evie in town is a second chance for all of us."

Three

EVIE STARED AT the battered ledger that served as a scheduling calendar. While Miss Monica had been a pleasant enough person and a good teacher, she hadn't believed in any invention that surfaced after 1960. The Smithsonian had been calling to ask if their old computer could be put on display in the history of technology section and the answering machine had to be from the 1980s. The worn tape had contained a single message that morning. Dominique Guérin, the new owner, had returned Evie's call. Her response to Evie's slightly panicked info dump about the loss of the head instructor and the upcoming ballet, about which Evie knew nothing, had been a cheerful "I have every confidence in you, my dear. I can't wait to see the production on Christmas Eve."

"Great," Evie said, clutching her mug of tea in her hands and willing her heart to stop beating at hummingbird speed. She felt as if she were trapped in some old black-and-white movie. "Come on, boys and girls. Let's put on a show!"

Only there was no production staff waiting in the shadows to work the cinematic magic. There was her, a battered ledger and sheer force of will. Oh, and sixty students she wasn't willing to disappoint.

She picked up her purse and crossed to the small mirror on the wall. After brushing her hair, she separated it into two sections and braided each one. She expertly wrapped the braids around her head and pinned them in place, then returned her purse to the desk drawer. Now she was ready to dance.

She heard footsteps on the stairs leading up to the studio. A few seconds later, a smiling woman with brown hair hurried into the reception area. Evie recognized her as one of the mothers but had no idea of her name.

"I'm running late," she proclaimed, handing Evie three CDs in cases. "Here's what you need. I hope. I mean I know it's what you wanted, I just hope they help."

The woman was in her late twenties, pretty, wearing a long-sleeved T-shirt with a large embroidered cartoon turkey on the front.

The woman laughed. "You look blank. I'm Patience McGraw. Lillie's mother."

"Oh. Lillie. Sure." Sweet girl with absolutely no talent, Evie thought. But she loved dancing and worked hard. Sometimes that was more important than ability.

"Charlie called me," Patience continued. "OMG, to quote my daughter. Miss Monica ran off with a man? I haven't been on a date in maybe three years, but my daughter's seventy-year-old dance teacher gets lucky? I can't decide if I should be depressed or inspired."

"I'm both," Evie admitted. "Slightly more depressed, though."

"Tell me about it." Patience gave a rueful laugh. "Anyway, Charlie explained that you're feeling completely abandoned and pressured. I can't help with the dance stuff. Lillie inherited her lack of coordination from me, I'm afraid. But I'm good at getting things done. So those are recordings of previous years' shows. One is mine. The other two come from other mothers. They're also for different years. I thought that might help."

Evie tightened her hold on the CDs. Right now, these were her best shot at figuring out what the program was supposed to look like.

"Thank you. You've saved me."

Patience laughed. "I'm barely getting started." She pulled a piece of paper out of her jeans's front pocket. "My phone number. I'll help get the work party together for the sets. Charlie mentioned those, too. So, a Saturday would work best. I suggest the first Saturday in December. All that's going on in town is the tree lighting and that's not until dusk. We'd have all day to spruce and paint and do whatever needs doing."

Evie took the paper with her free hand. In addition to Patience's phone number was a man's name.

"This guy is your contact at the hardware store in town. Tell him who you are and what you need the supplies for. He'll give you a great discount. Once you get that coordinated, get back to me and I'll spread the word about the work party. Oh, we'll also need to coordinate for the costumes."

Evie felt as if she were being pushed by an out-of-control tide. "You sew?"

"Enough to repair a costume. But I have the names of the talented ladies who do the real work. Plus, we need to schedule the fittings and then the run-through for hair and makeup." She drew in a breath and planted her hands on her hips. "Drat. There's one more thing that I can't... Brunch!" She grinned. "Thanksgiving morning we all meet at Jo's Bar. We have yummy brunch food, enough champagne so that we don't care about the turkey we're cooking and we watch the parade on TV. Girls only. You have to come. It's really fun. After we're stuffed and drunk, we head outside to watch the Fool's Gold parade through town."

"Okay," Evie said slowly, still overwhelmed by names, promises and information.

"Be there at nine." Patience pulled her phone

out of her pocket and glanced at the screen. "I'm running late. Nothing new, right? I have to get back to work. Call me with any questions." She started for the door. "And pick a date for the work party. We need to claim our labor."

Evie stood in the center of her studio. She was holding three CD cases and a small piece of paper, but she would swear she'd been buried under a giant mound of boxes or something. She tucked the CD cases into her purse. Tonight she would watch the recordings and start to make notes. As for the rest of it, she would have to sort through all she'd learned and make up some kind of schedule. She still wasn't convinced about the work party, but maybe a few parents would be willing to help.

She walked into the main studio and settled in front of the barre. A half hour or so of practice would settle her mind for the lessons to come. Slowly, carefully, conscious of her still-healing leg, she began to warm up. Two minutes later, her cell phone rang.

She straightened, slid her right foot back to the floor and walked over to where the phone sat on the reception desk.

The calling number was unfamiliar.

"Hello?"

"Evie? Hi, it's Heidi."

Heidi was Rafe's new wife. She lived on the

ranch and raised goats. A pretty blonde who had welcomed Evie with genuine warmth.

"Hi," Evie said, more cautious than excited about contact with her family.

"I wanted to make sure you knew we were having dinner at four on Thanksgiving. Rafe couldn't remember if you'd been told." Heidi sighed. "Men. Because social details aren't that interesting to them, right?"

Thanksgiving dinner? Evie held in a groan. She wasn't up to dinner with her relatives.

"Oh, and that morning we watch the parade at Jo's Bar. You know about that, right? It's a huge crowd. Girls only brunch. You'll love it. It's a great chance to meet everyone. Just be careful. The champagne goes down way too easy. Last year I had to call my grandfather to drive me home. I vowed I wasn't touching the stuff this year and I'm holding myself to that. Oh, it's on a local channel that starts the replay at nine our time. Just so you don't freak out and think you have to get up too early."

Evie heard a crash in the background.

Heidi gasped. "I think that was my new batch of cheese. I gotta run. Save the date."

The phone went silent.

Evie slowly pushed the end button, then replaced the phone in her bag and set the bag in the bottom drawer. As far as Heidi was concerned,

Evie had just accepted both invitations. Calling back to say no would mean answering questions and coming up with a reason why she wasn't joining the only people she knew in a town she'd just moved to. Talk about awkward.

In truth, she didn't mind spending time with her brothers. With new wives and fiancées hanging around, Evie should find it easy enough to avoid her mother.

She glanced at the clock on the wall, then walked to the stairs. Once she was on the main floor, she stepped into her brother's offices and moved toward Dante's desk. He was staring at his computer screen but glanced up as she approached.

"Hey," she said. "I wanted to warn you that tonight there's more clog dancing. No tap classes until tomorrow. Ballet the rest of the time. Ballet is quieter. Except for the music. But you seem to have this thing against the clog girls, so I'm letting you know in advance."

Dante sat at his desk, his blue eyes fixed on her, the oddest expression on his face.

"What?" she demanded, raising her hands to her head to make sure her braids were tightly in place.

He swore under his breath. "Is it legal?"

"Clog dancing? The last time I checked."

He opened his mouth, then closed it. "What you're wearing."

She glanced down at herself. She had on black

tights and a leotard. It was exactly what she wore nearly every day of her life. Scuffed ballet shoes covered her feet. Later, she would put on toe shoes to demonstrate some steps, but she wasn't going to walk around in them. She found that awkward and, okay, a little pretentious.

She pulled at the stretchy material. "It's worn, I'll admit, but I'm dressed."

Dante glanced around, as if checking to see who was watching them. As far as Evie could tell, everyone else was busy with work.

"You're practically naked."

She laughed. "I'm fully covered."

"Technically. But..." He waved his hand up and down in front of her body. "Shouldn't you put on a coat?"

She didn't understand. "Because why?"

"You're distracting."

"Really?"

"Look around. Do you see anyone else wearing an outfit like that?"

"It's not office wear."

He seemed a little glazed and frantic. For a second she allowed herself to believe he found her sexy. Wouldn't that be nice?

"You're killing me," he muttered.

She smiled. "That's so lovely. Thank you."

"You're welcome. Oh, the guy at the hardware store called me about the set."

"What? Why would he call you?"

"Because Charlie told him to. She has this idea that you don't know squat about construction."

"I don't, but it's my responsibility anyway." She was going to make sure her students weren't disappointed.

"Yeah, well, now I'm going to help, too. I thought we could go look at the sets together, and I'll put together a list of what needs doing."

She took a step back. "No, thanks. I appreciate the offer, but no."

"Why not?"

"Because, um, you're busy." Lame, but it was better than the truth. She wasn't willing to risk getting sucked in. Dante was pretty tempting. Handsome, funny, interesting. Sexy. Hard to resist.

"Why not?" he repeated.

She sighed. "You're my brother's business partner. I'm not looking to get more involved with my family. We have a long, complicated history. I won't bore you with it, but believe me when I say, stay far, far away."

He studied her. "Interesting. A mystery. I love a good mystery."

"Don't be intrigued. I'm a seriously boring person. You're sweet to offer, but no. I'll do it myself."

His phone rang. He swore quietly. "I have to take this call, but our conversation isn't over."

He couldn't be more wrong, she thought, giving

a cheerful wave and hurrying away. Dante was a complication she didn't need and couldn't afford. Him being nice would make staying away more difficult, but even more necessary.

THE OFFICE CLEARED OUT a little after five. Dante kept working. Right on time, the thudding of clog-clad feet pounded above his head. He turned off his computer and ducked out while he could. But an hour later he returned and made his way upstairs. Evie was turning out the lights in the studio, obviously done for the night.

She turned and looked at him, her expression slightly guarded. He took in her bulky sweatshirt and fitted jeans, and raised his eyebrows.

"You changed."

She pointed at him. "You did, too."

"I don't think my suit would get the same reaction as your work clothes."

"I don't know," she told him. "I do love a man in a tie."

"Now you're just messing with me."

"You make it easy."

Her eyes were big and green, with dark lashes. He would guess she wasn't wearing much in the way of makeup, which was fine by him. He liked women in all shapes and sizes. From high-maintenance divas to the most casual of tree-huggers.

"I'm going to help you with the sets," he said. "You can accept gracefully or you can fight me, but in the end, I'll win. I always win."

"Doing your civic duty?"

"Helping out a friend."

He liked her. She was Rafe's sister. As for the way she looked in dance clothes, that was his problem alone. He knew better than to go down dangerous paths.

He thought briefly of his mother, how she would have liked Evie and adored the little girls who danced. His mother had wanted so much more than the hardscrabble life she'd been forced to deal with. She'd wanted him to be a success. She would be happy about that, too.

Knowing her, she would accept the price she'd had to pay to get him on the right road. Something he could never accept or forgive in himself. He supposed that made her the better person. Hardly a surprise.

"It's Christmas," he said. "Think of this as me getting in the spirit."

"You don't like Christmas spirit."

"Maybe helping you will change my mind." He shrugged. "You know you can't do it alone. Accept the inevitable and say thank you."

She drew in a breath. "I know I can't do it alone, and for what it's worth, I trust you."

"I think there's a compliment buried in there."

"There is. Thank you."

He smiled. "Was that so hard?"

"You have no idea."

"Then while you're still wrestling with your personal growth, let me add, your brother invited me to Thanksgiving dinner." He braced himself for her rant.

"Good. I was hoping for a big crowd."

Unexpected, he thought. "Should I ask why?"

"No. You should assume I'm just one of those friendly types who loves humanity."

"Your recent resistance to me helping aside." He leaned against her desk.

"Yes."

"And your feelings on humanity?"

"Okay in small groups." She held up a piece of paper. "I was visited earlier by one of the moms. Patience. She swears there really can be a work party to restore my sets."

"Good. We'll make the list of what needs fixing and get it organized."

He studied her. From what he could tell, she wore her hair up for her lessons—two braids wrapped around her head. But now, with her work done for the day, she'd left it loose. Wavy strands of honey-blond hair fell past her shoulders and halfway down her back.

He would bet she had soft hair, he thought, imagining her bending over him. He could practically feel the cool silk in his fingers. She would be all muscle, he thought absently. Long legs. Incredibly flexible.

"Dante?"

He blinked himself back into the room. "Sorry."

She tilted her head, her mouth curving into a smile. "Want to tell me where you went?"

"Nope."

"Are you going to help me?" She paused. "Go with me to look at the sets?"

Was that what they'd been talking about? "Sure. When do you want to do that?"

"You weren't listening at all, were you?"

"Not even a little."

"At least you're honest about it." She folded her arms across her chest. "Now. I suggested we go now."

"Works for me." He studied her, wondering how much trouble he would get in for kissing her, and knowing it would be worth it. "Here's the thing."

She raised her eyebrows. "You're putting conditions on helping me? You're the one who insisted."

"No. I'm telling you that when I said I was a player, I wasn't kidding. I never get serious. I don't do relationships and I'm not the guy you take home to meet the parents."

"You're already having dinner with my mother on Thanksgiving."

"That's different. It's not a date."

She tilted her head. "You're warning me off."

"Yes."

"I haven't expressed any interest in you. Is this your ego talking? Are you assuming that a woman can't be in the same room with you without begging for your attention?"

"I wish, but, no."

Her gaze was steady. "You're going to make a move."

"Most likely."

One corner of her mouth turned up. "Announcing it up front isn't exactly smooth."

"You're difficult to resist."

She laughed. "Oh, please. I'm very resistible. Trust me."

He moved a little closer. He liked the sound of her laughter and how she wasn't aware of her appeal.

She put her hand on his chest. "Let me see if I have this straight. You're warning me that you're not someone I want to be involved with, and at the same time, you're convinced you have enough going for you that I'll give in anyway."

"Absolutely."

He put his hand on hers, liking the feel of her fingers against his chest. Skin on skin would be better, but a man had to take what he could get.

She pulled free and dropped her arm to her side,

then shook her head. "You're a weird guy, you know that?"

"I've been called worse."

"I'm sure you have. Let me get my coat, and while we head to the warehouse, you can share all the details. Knowing the depth of your awfulness will help me resist you."

"Now you're mocking me."

"Hey, you think you can seduce me against my will. I think a little mocking is called for."

Four

EVIE WASN'T SURE about brunch at a bar, but she showed up right on time anyway. She was a little bleary-eyed from spending every free moment over the past few days watching the videos of *The Dance of the Winter King.* She'd broken down the choreography of over half of the production. With luck, by the end of the holiday weekend, she would have the whole dance down on paper and then be able to put it all together for the girls.

While each age group had already learned the basic steps they would need for their section of the production, there were no transitions, no flow and the order of the dances had yet to be determined. Traditionally, the younger, less experienced students would go first, but Evie was playing with the idea of having the older soloists do short routines in between each group. Although, with time ticking, that might not be a smart move.

She walked into Jo's Bar to find the main room

already filled with a couple of dozen women. Unlike regular bars she'd been to, this one had flattering lighting, the TVs already tuned to the parade and the smell of cinnamon and vanilla filling the air.

The bar itself was being used as a buffet. Large chafing dishes sat in a row, with a stack of plates at one end. Big trays of cut up fresh fruit offered healthy choices next to a display of pastries that made Evie's mouth water. Even the voice in her head—the one that warned about potential butt and thigh growth—was silent with carb anticipation.

A tall no-nonsense thirtysomething woman walked over carrying a tray of glasses of champagne. She stopped in front of Evie.

"I don't know you," she said, a friendly smile buffering her blunt statement. "Visiting relatives?"

"Evie Stryker."

The woman's eyes widened. "The mysterious dancing sister of the cowboy brothers. Everyone wants to meet you."

"I can't decide if that's a compliment or if it makes me sound like the villain in a horror movie."

The woman laughed. "Dancer killer. I like it. I'm Jo, by the way. This is my bar." She nodded toward a guy opening bottles of champagne behind the bar. "I promised everyone this would be girls only, but he's married to me, so technically he doesn't count. Besides, he's a good guy, so that's something. Your group is over at that table. Enjoy."

Evie walked in the direction Jo had indicated, not sure what she would find. Heidi, Annabelle and Charlie were already there, which allowed her to relax.

Annabelle, Shane's pregnant fiancée, jumped to her feet when she spotted Evie. "Thank goodness. Charlie is not willing to drink for two, which is very selfish of her, and Heidi's resisting drinking at all."

"I have to handle dinner later," Heidi protested. "I'm responsible for the turkey. Do you really want me wielding a sharp knife after a couple of glasses of champagne? I don't think so. If I hurt myself, one of you will have to milk the goats."

Annabelle sighed. "Fine. Be reasonable." She drew Evie to the table. "I'm dying for champagne. Can you drink a glass now so I can watch you and experience it vicariously? Please?"

"Ah, sure," Evie said, not clear on what Annabelle wanted. She didn't think watching someone else drink would be very satisfying, but she was willing to go along with it.

She sipped from the glass Annabelle handed her. "Delicious."

Annabelle sighed. "I knew it. I miss champagne."

"I'd miss coffee more," Charlie muttered. "The

whole pregnancy thing is a giant pain in the ass, if you ask me."

"It's not really your ass that hurts," Annabelle said in a mock whisper.

Charlie rolled her eyes. "Thanks for the update."

"I thought you were hearing the pitter-patter of little feet," Heidi said.

Charlie ran her hands through her cropped hair. "We're still negotiating." The strong, competent firefighter flushed. "Clay is worried that once I'm pregnant we're going to have to, um, spend less time…you know. He wants a few more months of us alone."

Evie stared at her, not sure what she was talking about. Wouldn't they still be alone during the pregnancy?

Annabelle leaned toward her. "Sex. She's talking about sex. Clay's worried that Charlie might have morning sickness or something and he won't be getting as much. They need the bloom to wear off the rose, so to speak."

Evie covered her ears. "Okay, I'm not having that conversation. Clay's my brother and that's just disgusting."

The other three laughed.

Conversation shifted to the plans for the day— what was happening when. The four of them walked over to get started on the buffet.

"Oh, Dante said he'd drive you, if you want,"

Heidi told Evie. "He said to knock on his door when you were ready."

"Thanks."

She hadn't seen Dante since their trip to the warehouse a couple of days before. Despite the flirtatious teasing at the dance studio, once they'd arrived to view the sets, he'd been all business. His claims to have worked in construction had turned out to be true. He'd studied the sets, had taken notes on what needed to be fixed and started a preliminary supply list.

All things that would help, Evie told herself. She had a big job ahead of her, and she didn't have the time to complicate her life with a guy. Still, there was something about Dante....

Something best left unexplored, she cautioned herself. A philosophy he obviously embraced. For all his flirty ways, after the set viewing, he'd simply dropped her off at her place with a quick goodbye and left. Apparently the only thing he'd exaggerated had been his attraction to her.

Evie collected a small piece of stuffed French toast and some bacon. Heidi chose a lot of protein, while Charlie filled her plate with food for twenty. Annabelle kept touching her stomach, as if trying to figure out what she and the baby were in the mood for.

Five women walked in together, and most of

those already in the bar called out greetings. Heidi moved close to Evie.

"The Hendrix family women," she murmured. "Denise is the mother. The three who look exactly alike are triplets. Dakota, Montana and Nevada. Nevada's the one who's pregnant. The one who doesn't look like the others is Liz Sutton, the writer. She's married to Denise's oldest son."

The women looked happy to be together, Evie thought, watching them. The sisters and sister-in-law seemed especially close and kept near their mom.

She knew her brothers had grown up tight and, even when Rafe was at his most imperious, had kept in touch with the other brothers. She'd always been the odd one out. Never fitting in. As a kid, she'd felt as if everyone was mad at her all the time, but she never knew why.

She started back to the table, only to come to a stop in front of her mother.

"Hello, Evie," May said with a tentative smile.

"Um, hi. I didn't know you were going to be here."

"I drove in after Heidi. I wanted to get a few things started for dinner tonight."

Evie nodded, wondering if her sister-in-law had known May was coming to the brunch all along, but had failed to mention it. Had Heidi made that clear, Evie would have found a reason not to attend.

Evie started to step around her. May put her hand on her arm.

"Wait," her mother said. "Evie, we should talk." May glanced around at the crowded bar. "Maybe not here. But soon."

Evie looked for a place to set down her plate. She'd suddenly lost her appetite. "There's not very much for us to talk about."

"Of course there is. It's been so long. I want…" May drew in a breath. "I'd like us to stop being angry with each other."

To anyone else, that was probably a very reasonable statement. Evie fought against the sudden rush of tears in her eyes. "Sure. But first answer me a question. What do you have to be mad about? Me being born? Because that's not anything I could control."

May stiffened. "That came out wrong. I'm sorry."

Evie shook her head. "I don't think it came out wrong at all. I think you've been angry with me for a long time. As for talking, as far as I'm concerned, until you can tell me what it is you think I did, we have nothing to say to each other."

With that she walked back to the table. She set down her plate, picked up her champagne glass and drained it. Then she went in search of a refill.

"ARE YOU DRUNK?" Dante asked.

Evie leaned back into the soft leather of his very expensive, very German car. She'd been driving the same dented, slightly rusty old Chevy for nearly five years. The seats were more spring than foam, the windows didn't close right and the mechanic actually sighed every time she took her car in for service.

"This is nice," she said, stroking the side of the heated seat. "I'll try not to throw up."

"Gee, thanks," Dante said, turning his attention back to the road. "You *are* drunk."

"I'm buzzed. There's a difference."

"It's one in the afternoon."

"I was at a brunch and there was champagne. Plus I had a fight with my mom and that took away my appetite." She frowned, or at least tried to. She couldn't exactly feel her forehead. "We didn't fight. Not really. She said we should stop being mad at each other. I'm the kid. What did I ever do? That's what I asked. Is she pissed I was born? But she didn't have an answer. There's never a good reason, you know?"

She turned to Dante and blinked. "What were we talking about?"

"You need to eat something."

"Turkey. I'll eat turkey."

"That'll help." He glanced at her. "She said she was angry?"

Evie tried to remember May's exact words. "She said she would like us to stop being angry at each other. Being annoyed at me is kind of implied."

"Poor kid." Dante briefly put his hand on top of hers.

For a second Evie enjoyed the warmth of the contact, then the meaning of his words sank into her slightly soggy brain. Poor kid? Poor *kid?* Is that how he saw her? As a child? What happened to her being a sexy vixen? Not that he'd ever used that phrase, but still. He'd implied she was. Or at least her dancer work clothes. She didn't want to be a kid. She wanted to be vixeny. Vixenish. Whatever.

She leaned her head back against the seat and sighed. Life was far from fair.

Two hours later she'd munched her way through a fair amount of the veggie platter Heidi had put out and finished off about a half gallon of water. The buzz was long gone, as was the faint headache that had followed. Through careful maneuvering, she'd managed to avoid spending any time alone with her mother. Oddly enough, Dante had helped more than a little. He'd stuck beside her from the second they walked in the door.

Painfully aware that his concern was more fraternal than she would like, she told herself not to read anything into his actions. Dante was practically family. There was no way to avoid him while she was in Fool's Gold, and as her plans had her staying well into the new year, logic needed to win over longing. Well, not longing. Acknowledging that Dante was smart and sexy was simply stating the obvious. It wasn't as if she had a thing for him or wanted anything other than casual friendship.

"Halftime," Heidi said, walking into the living room. "It's time, people."

"Time for what?" Dante asked.

"I have no idea," Evie admitted, but stood along with everyone else.

Shane sighed. "It's Thanksgiving."

Evie pointed to the kitchen. "You know, the big turkey in the oven was our first clue."

"Funny. It's Thanksgiving, and if we get a big feast, so do the animals," Shane said.

Dante groaned. "Including the elephant?"

"Especially the elephant. My racehorses have a very controlled diet, but everybody else gets a treat. Do you know what a watermelon costs this time of year?"

They all followed Shane and Heidi outside where a truck waited. The back of the pickup was filled with all kinds of holiday goodies. There was the massive watermelon for Priscilla, the elephant, carrots and apples for the goats, Reno, the pony, Wilbur, the pig, and the riding horses. Something from the local butcher for the feral cat who had taken up residence with Priscilla and Reno.

Evie and Dante were assigned the riding horses.

"You know what you're doing?" Shane asked.

Evie sniffed. "Yes. We'll be fine."

They walked toward the corral. Six horses trotted over to greet them. Dante hesitated.

"They have really big teeth," he said. "You're okay with that?"

She smiled. "Keep your fingers away from their teeth and you'll be fine."

She took the knife Heidi had provided and sliced the apple in quarters, then put a piece on her hand, straightened her fingers so her palm was flat and offered it to the first horse. He took it gently, his lips barely brushing her skin.

"Impressive," Dante said and did the same with another quarter of apple.

"Look out!" she yelled, just as the horse reached for him.

He jumped back, dropping the apple piece. "What?"

She grinned. "Nothing. Just messing with you."

"Charming." He took another piece of apple and held it out to the horse. "Sorry about that," he said. "You know women."

"Um, you're talking to a girl horse."

"She understands just fine."

They finished giving the horses their holiday treats, then headed back to the house. When they stepped onto the porch, Dante paused. "Did you grow up here?"

Evie looked out at the rolling hills of the ranch. The air was cool, but the sky blue. To the east, snow-capped mountains rose toward the sun.

"Technically I was born in Fool's Gold," she admitted. "But I don't remember much about it. We moved when I was pretty young."

Her earliest memories were of the tiny apartment they'd had in Los Angeles. The three boys had been crammed into the larger of the two bedrooms. May had taken the smaller bedroom for herself and Evie had slept on the sofa.

"Are you happy to be back?"

"I like teaching dance," she said, willing to admit that much of the truth. "I wasn't sure I would, but it's gratifying. The girls are enthusiastic and excited to learn." A few were talented, but she'd discovered she was less interested in skill than attitude when it came to her students.

"Let me guess," he said, glancing at her. "The clog dancing is your favorite."

She laughed. "It's a very important art form."

"It's loud and on top of my head."

For a second she allowed herself to get lost in his dark blue eyes. Then common sense took over, and she gave him her best sympathetic smile. "It's for the children, Dante. Not everything is about you."

"It should be," he grumbled. "Come on. The second half is starting."

"You know, I was run over by a football player only a few months ago. Does it occur to you that watching the game could be traumatic?"

"Is it?"

"No. I'm just saying it could be."

He wrapped his arm around her and drew her inside. "Stay close. I'll protect you."

For a second she allowed herself to believe he wasn't just being funny. That he was someone she could depend on. She knew better, of course. Her family had taught her that the people who were supposed to love you back usually didn't and that it was far safer to simply be alone. She was done with love.

DINNER WAS MORE ENJOYABLE than Evie had allowed herself to hope was possible. With ten people sitting around a large table, it was easy to avoid awkward silences and difficult questions. Even more fortunate, May had sat at the opposite end, on the same side, so Evie didn't have to try to avoid her at all.

Once everyone had eaten their fill of turkey, dressing, mashed potatoes, sweet potato casserole, vegetables, olives, rolls and a very confusing Jell-O mold, conversation turned to the holiday season in Fool's Gold.

"You pretty much need a schedule of events on the refrigerator," Charlie was saying. "The town starts decorating this weekend. Next Saturday night is the tree lighting."

Heidi leaned against Rafe. "We're doing hay-rides."

Dante turned to her. "What?"

Shane groaned. "Hayrides. Horses pulling sleighs." He glanced out at the rapidly darkening night. "Or wagons if we don't get snow."

Evie knew he sounded exasperated but guessed it was all an act. Shane liked everything about the ranch, including the close proximity to town. More important to him was how Annabelle enjoyed the holidays.

She glanced around the table, startled to realize all her relatives were paired up. A year ago everyone had been single. Since the last holiday season, Rafe and May had both married and Shane and Clay had gotten engaged. Annabelle was pregnant. This time next year Shane and Annabelle would have their baby. Heidi and Charlie would probably *be* pregnant, and she would be gone.

"I ate too much," Glen, May's husband, said as he pushed back from the table. "Wonderful dinner. Thank you."

May smiled at him. "It wasn't just me. Everyone helped."

"Not me," Evie said, suddenly wanting a few minutes away from her family. "So I insist on cleaning up. Everyone carry your plates into the kitchen, then leave me to it."

"You can't do all the dishes yourself," Heidi said.

"There's a brand-new dishwasher that says otherwise," Evie told her.

"I'll help," Dante said. "I'm good at taking orders."

"We all know that's not true," Rafe said. "But, hey, if he wants to wash, I say let him."

It only took a few minutes to clear the table. Heidi took charge of the leftovers and put them neatly away in the refrigerator, then Evie shooed her out so she could start rinsing the dishes. As promised, Dante stayed behind and began stacking serving pieces.

May walked in. "I want to help."

Evie forced a smile. "You made most of the dinner. I can handle this."

Her mother stared at her. "You really hate me, don't you?"

Evie felt her shoulders slump. "Mom, it's Thanksgiving. Why do you have to make me helping with cleanup more than it is?"

"Because you've been avoiding me." She pressed her lips together. "I know you had a difficult childhood and it's my fault. It's just that you…" Tears filled her eyes, and she looked away.

Evie told herself to be sympathetic. That nothing would be gained by snapping or complaining. There was no new material here. Just the same half-truths and partial explanations.

May sniffed. "Can't you forgive me?"

Evie folded her arms across her chest in what she knew was a protective and not very subtle gesture. "Sure. You're forgiven."

"You're still angry." May drew in a breath. "I know I wasn't there for you, when you were little. There were so many responsibilities."

"I'm sure it was difficult to raise four children on your own," Evie told her. "But we both know that's not the problem. The problem is you had a one-night stand a few months after your husband died, and I'm the result. The problem is, every time you look at me, you're reminded of your moment of weakness. You never wanted me, and, growing up, you made sure I knew it. It's not enough that I don't even know who my father is. I ended up with a mother who didn't give a damn."

May clutched at her throat. "That's not true."

"Isn't it? You blamed me for being born. That's my big crime. When I was little, you wanted nothing to do with me. You were never there for me. You weren't overtly mean, but you also weren't interested. You and my brothers had special things you did together. Rituals and celebrations. Things I wasn't a part of. It was the four of you as a family and then me on the outside looking in. My brothers did their best with me, but it wasn't their job to raise me. It was yours and you didn't bother."

Evie felt herself starting to shake. She tried to hold it all together but knew she was seconds from a complete meltdown.

"I left home as soon as I could because there was no reason to stay. I never wanted to come back and wouldn't be here now if you and my brothers hadn't literally brought me here while I was unconscious after the accident." She almost blurted out that she wasn't planning on staying, either, but May didn't deserve to know her plans. She wouldn't be a part of her future.

"I was seventeen when I took off, and it was over a year until I heard from you. You never checked on me or wondered where I was or what I was doing."

"You were at Juilliard," May whispered.

"Right. For the first six months. Then I left. Did you ever wonder how a seventeen-year-old girl makes it on her own in the world? Did you bother to ask?"

The room blurred, and it took her a minute to realize she was crying.

"So, sure, Mom," she said, her voice thickening. "I forgive you. You were everything I ever wanted in a parent."

Then she was running. She went out through the back porch and down the stairs. Somewhere along the path to the goat barn, she stumbled and nearly fell. The only thing that kept her from going down was a pair of strong arms.

Dante pulled her against him and held her tight. He didn't say anything. He just hung on and let her sob until she had nothing left.

Five

DANTE WAS SURPRISED to find Rafe in the office Friday morning. "Why aren't you home with Heidi?" he asked.

Rafe looked up from his computer. "She's making cheese and let me know I was getting in her way. Figured I'd get some work done. What about you?"

"Heidi pretty much only has eyes for you."

Rafe chuckled. "I'm lucky that way."

Dante walked to his desk and turned on his computer, then poured himself a cup of coffee. They were the only two working that morning. The staff had been given the long weekend off.

"How's your mom?" Dante asked.

"Fine. Why?"

Dante had wondered if May had told anyone what had happened. He'd let Evie cry herself out, then had driven her home. This morning he'd wanted to go check on her, but there'd been no sign she was awake when he'd left.

He'd been forced to walk away, still feeling protective but with nothing to do.

"She and Evie got into it last night," Dante said and recapped the conversation.

Rafe shifted uncomfortably in his chair. "I wish they wouldn't talk about the past. There's nothing that can be done to fix it."

"Was Evie telling the truth?" Dante asked. "Was she that isolated as a kid?"

"It was complicated," Rafe admitted. "She was a lot younger, and I think she was a reminder of that one night for my mom. The four of us were used to being together, then Evie came along...." His voice trailed off.

Dante had lost his mother when he'd been fifteen. While he hadn't been the one to pull the trigger, a case could be made that he was responsible. They'd always been there for each other, and to this day, he would give anything to have her back. He couldn't comprehend what it would be like to have family and not be close to them.

"She's your sister," he began.

"I know." He sighed. "I was too busy being the man of the family. I figured the rest of them would worry about Evie. But that never happened. She was always an afterthought." He shook his head. "There's no excuse."

Dante had known Rafe a lot of years and trusted him completely. From what he'd seen, May was a sweet, loving person. So how had everyone managed to ignore what was going on with Evie?

"She's here now," Rafe continued. "We want to make things up to her."

"Good luck with that."

"You think she'll resist?"

"If you were her, how forgiving would you be?"

Rafe sighed. "Yeah, I see your point. I appreciate you looking out for her." He stared at Dante. "That's all it is, right? You're not getting involved?"

Dante knew exactly what his friend was asking. Telling Rafe he thought Evie was sexy as hell, from the way she walked to her hard-won smile, wasn't a smart move. Instead he settled on the truth.

"You know how I feel about relationships." In his world, love had deadly consequences. He'd learned the lesson early and had never let it go.

THE FRIDAY AFTER Thanksgiving wasn't a school day, so Evie had scheduled her dance classes early. She was done by three and showered, dressed and settled in front of her television by four. She pushed the play button on her remote, cuing up the DVD of the performance, then settled back on her sofa to watch it for the fortieth time.

The story was simple. The Winter King had dozens of daughters. The girls wanted to go free in the world, but he loved them too much to let them go. So his daughters danced to convince him they were ready to leave. At the end, the girls were revealed as beautiful snowflakes and he released them into the world as Christmas snow.

The girls danced in groups. They were mostly divided by age, with the younger performers having more simple choreography. Every student had a few seconds of a solo with the more advanced students having longer in the spotlight. Several styles of dance were represented. Modern, tap, clog and, of course, ballet.

The sets were simple, the lighting basic. The music was a collection of classic holiday songs, leaning heavily on Tchaikovsky. What would the world have done without his beautiful *Nutcracker?* The biggest problem in her mind was the transitions. They were awkward in some places, nonexistent in others. Sometimes the girls simply walked off the stage, and the next group walked on. Every time she watched that part of the performance, she winced.

Evie made a few notes, then rewound to the clog dancers who opened the show. Some of their steps were similar to tap, she thought. The sounds could echo each other. Slower, then faster. She stood and moved along with the girls on the recording. But as they turned to leave, she kept dancing, going a little more quickly, finding the rhythm of the tap dancers as they moved onto the stage.

She paused the frame and wrote some more, then made a couple of quick drawings to capture the exact poses she imagined. She moved on to the next transition and made changes there. She was just starting the third when someone rang her doorbell.

Her first thought was that it might be her mother. Dread coiled in her stomach. She wasn't ready to face May, to deal with the family trauma again. Was hiding and ignoring the interruption too cowardly?

Whoever was at the door rang the bell again. Reluctantly, she walked over and opened it.

Relief was instant. Dante stood on her doorstep. He smiled at her.

"You're home. I didn't hear any pounding above my head, so I thought maybe you'd finished early. Get your coat."

He looked good, she thought, studying his amused expression. He wore a leather jacket over jeans and a scarf. He had on boots. She could feel the cold of the rapidly darkening late afternoon.

She put her hands on her hips. "Get my coat? Was that an order? Newsflash. I don't work for you."

"Good. Because I don't take anyone on my staff

out." He sighed. "Seriously, you're going to be difficult?"

"No. I'm going to ask where we're going."

"Didn't I say 'out'? I would swear I did."

She laughed. "Out where?"

"To the center of town. They're decorating. Neither of us particularly likes the holiday season, so we need to be with people who are less corrupt. It will be good for us."

"Will it?" She stepped back to allow him inside. "When did you make this discovery?"

"Earlier. So are you coming or what?"

"Give me a second."

She turned off her TV and the laptop she'd hooked up for the DVDs, then stepped into boots and pulled them on. After shoving her house keys and a few dollars into her jeans pockets, she shrugged on her coat.

"I'm ready."

Dante stared at her. "Impressive. Less than two minutes."

"You've never had to change costumes during a performance of *Swan Lake*."

"That's true. How perceptive of you."

They walked outside. She locked the door, then followed him to the sidewalk.

The couple across the street was putting up Christmas lights. Several other townhouses had wreathes on doors and lights twinkling from doors and rooftops.

"We're really going into town?" she asked.

"Yes. The whole place has transformed."

"I noticed a few Christmas decorations being put up this morning," she admitted, "but nothing that earth-shattering."

He took her hand in his. "You walked home the back way, didn't you? Through the residential part of town."

"Uh-huh."

His fingers were warm and strong next to hers. His skin smooth without being too soft. She couldn't remember the last time she'd held hands with a guy. This was nice, she told herself. She and Dante weren't dating—she wasn't that stupid. She knew better than to fall for her brother's business partner. But some gentle flirting, a little handsome male company, wasn't going to hurt anyone.

"You'd be amazed what this town can do in a day," he told her.

"You sound impressed."

"You will be, too. How's the dance prep coming? I heard the clog dancers earlier."

She laughed. "Sorry about that. I don't know how to make it quiet."

"I'm getting used to the noise and they're getting better."

"How can you tell?"

"They're more rhythmic."

"That's true. At least most of the students are studying ballet. It's quieter."

"Unless they fall."

She winced, remembering the mass tumble during her two o'clock class. "You heard that?"

"It registered as a minor earthquake. The local seismology office called to see if we were okay."

She shoved him in the arm. "It wasn't that bad."

"They didn't do it on your head."

"Smug lawyer type," she grumbled. "They're learning. It doesn't always go well."

"I didn't say it had to stop. I'm looking forward to seeing the performance."

"You'll be intimately familiar with the music." She glanced at him. "Will you really come see the show? Won't you be off visiting family?"

"There's just me."

"What about your dad?"

"I never knew him."

"I didn't know mine, either. But you probably guessed that from the slight altercation you witnessed yesterday."

He drew her close and kissed her cheek. "It sucks."

The blunt assessment was oddly comforting. "It does," she admitted. "Hey, I don't know anything about you."

"I like being mysterious. Sort of a James Bond of the lawyer set."

She laughed. "Hardly. So tell me something interesting."

"That's too much pressure. Ask me a question."

"Have you ever been arrested?"

"Yes."

She stopped on the sidewalk and stared at him. "Seriously?"

"More than once."

"You went to jail?"

"I served time."

"No way. You can't have a criminal record and be a lawyer."

"Pretty and smart," he told her. "That makes you irresistible. Okay, you're right. I was a juvenile. My records were expunged."

"What did you do?"

His normally open expression tightened. "Bad stuff. I was in a gang."

Evie tried to imagine the well-dressed, smooth man next to her as a kid in a gang. Her imagination wasn't that good. Before she could figure out what else to ask, he tugged her along and they turned a corner, entering one of the main streets of Fool's Gold.

Just yesterday the stores and windows had featured turkeys and pumpkins. Any lights had been orange, and garlands had been made of leaves. In the space of a few hours, the transformation to the Christmas holidays had begun.

Baskets of holiday greens with shiny silver and red decorations hung from the lampposts. The windows were now covered with painted holiday displays—pictures of wrapped packages or snowmen, a few nutcrackers. Morgan's Books had stacks of popular children's books on tables and a sign promising Santa would be coming to read *'Twas the Night Before Christmas* next Saturday, after the town Christmas tree lighting.

Up ahead, in the main square, a large crane was being attached to the biggest live Christmas tree Evie had ever seen in real life. It had to be twenty feet tall.

"But it was Thanksgiving yesterday," she said, feeling as if she was going to see snow and Dickens carolers any second.

"Tell me about it," Dante told her. "There's more."

He led her toward the center of town, past the tree on the flatbed. Booths had been set up selling everything from hot chocolate to pizza slices.

"Because nothing says the holidays like pepperoni?" she asked.

Dante grinned. "Come on. I'll buy you a slice."

They got pizza and soda and walked over to watch the tree being secured by thick chains before being raised into place. The scent of pine filled the air. The pizza was hot and gooey and more calories than Evie usually allowed herself in a day.

She wasn't a professional dancer anymore, she reminded herself. Or a cheerleader. She could afford to have a BMI over twenty.

Families crowded around them. She recognized one of the women from the brunch yesterday morning, but couldn't remember her name. She was a pretty blonde, with an adorable toddler in her arms. Her husband held a baby boy.

The little girl pointed to the tree slowly rising from the truck bed. "We have one like that?" she asked.

Her father chuckled. "Sorry, Hannah. Our ceiling isn't that high. But we'll pick out a good tree. You'll see."

The woman leaned into her husband. They shared a look—one that spoke of love and promise. Aware she'd caught a glimpse of something private, Evie turned away.

Back when she'd still been young enough to believe in miracles, she'd assumed she would find love and have a family. That one day a man would promise to be with her forever. She would belong, and that belonging would finally heal her.

Several bad boyfriends later, she was less sure love was something she could count on and more convinced people who were supposed to love you usually didn't. She wanted to tell herself it could still happen, but she had a feeling that was just the Christmas tree talking.

She glanced toward Dante. "Thanks for your help yesterday. For getting me home and everything."

"No problem. Families can be complicated."

"My mom's a nightmare."

"It's not just her."

"You mean my brothers?"

Dante looked into her eyes. "Sure, they hold part of the blame, but so do you."

If they hadn't been in the middle of a crowd, she would have taken a step back. But more people had stopped to watch the tree put in place, and there was nowhere to go.

"Me? I'm the kid here."

"You were," Dante told her gently, his voice low. "You're an adult now, and if you want things to work out with your family, you have to make a little effort. Does keeping your mom at bay really make you happy? Don't you want more? A connection?"

She wanted to say no but remembered that he didn't have anyone. No doubt he would tell her to be careful what she wished for. He was the kind of man who would take care of people, only there wasn't anyone to watch over in his life. Right now, she had the benefit of his instincts.

"I like the theory of family," she admitted, "if

not the practice. It was so bad for so long, I don't know how to let go of the hurt."

"You take baby steps."

"I'd rather leave."

"Is that the plan?"

She nodded. "I like teaching dance. I think I want to continue that. I'm going to stick around for a while and learn all I can, while saving money. Then go open a studio somewhere else."

She braced herself for Dante's judgment, but he only nodded slowly. "That's an option."

"My family doesn't know."

"I won't say anything. How long's 'a while'?"

"Maybe a year." She wrinkled her nose. "Okay, okay, I get your point. That's long enough to try to work things out with my family. I should give them a break, or at least credit for trying."

He leaned in and kissed her nose. "See, it's like I said. Smart *and* pretty."

She shoved at his chest. "It's not a compliment when you're being annoying."

He chuckled and put his arm around her. They both watched as the tree was pulled upright, then slowly lowered into place. Everyone cheered.

Evie leaned into him, enjoying being a part of the happy crowd more than she would have thought.

When the tree was secure, Dante led her back toward the booths. "We need hot chocolate."

She shivered slightly. "I could use something warm."

He bought them each a cup and they checked out the rest of the booths. One of them was selling ornaments in bright colors.

"They come with your name painted on them," the woman in the booth said with a smile. "How about a lovely star?"

She held up a red one.

"We'll take it," Dante told her, then spelled Evie's name.

"I don't have a tree," she said.

"We'll get one of those later. You need an ornament with your name on it."

"Only if you get one, too."

"You going to let me put it on your tree?"

She laughed and leaned close. "Yes, but why does that question sound dirty?"

"Because it was supposed to."

They both laughed.

He paid for both ornaments and tucked the small bag into his coat pocket. They continued to wander through the center of town, then turned back toward their neighborhood.

Somewhere in the distance, a church clock chimed the hour. She could hear Christmas music. There were a thousand stars in the sky, and her breath made puffy clouds in the cold air.

"I'll admit it," she told him. "There is something

just a little magical about this place. The tree, the hot cocoa, the window decorations."

He stopped and faced her. "It's going to get worse."

"What do you mean?"

"Your family at the holidays? There are going to be a lot of get-togethers."

She could only imagine. "I tend to stay on the fringes. It's easier that way."

"You're assuming they'll let you. I think the easiest solution is practice."

She had no idea what he was talking about, but it didn't matter. Staring into Dante's blue eyes was kind of a nice way to spend an evening. She didn't even care that she was freezing.

"For example," he continued, his gaze locked with hers. "What if there's mistletoe somewhere? We'll be expected to kiss."

She felt herself smile. "Oh, right. That could be awkward. We barely know each other. What if we bump noses?"

"Our timing could be off. People would talk. I know you wouldn't want that."

"I wouldn't." Anticipation tiptoed through her stomach, warming her from the inside out. She tilted her head. "So you think we should practice?"

He sighed heavily. "It's probably for the best."

"You're such a giver."

"I am."

With that, he lowered his head and pressed his mouth to hers.

His lips were warm and tasted faintly of chocolate. He kissed gently, lingering as if he'd been waiting for this his whole day and planned to enjoy every second of it. She put her hand on his chest while he held her lightly by the waist.

They were on the edge of the main square, neatly tucked in a doorway to a closed shop. Around them twinkle lights flashed on and off. It was like something out of a Christmas movie, she thought, letting her eyes flutter shut as she concentrated on the heat burning through her.

They stayed there for what felt like a long time. While part of her wanted to deepen the kiss, another part was content to leave things as they were. Uncomplicated, with just enough zing to make her thighs tighten. The perfect combination, she thought hazily.

Dante drew back and rested his forehead on hers.

"I'd give us a B."

She opened her eyes and glared at him. "Excuse me?"

He grinned. "Kidding. That was nice. But we probably need more practice."

"What did you have in mind?"

"We have a month until Christmas. That gives us time to work out the kinks."

She laughed and linked arms with him. "You're the strangest man I know."

"That's what all the girls say. Admit it. You like me."

She laughed again, and they started for home. In truth, she did like Dante. She wasn't an idiot—she knew he was a player and that expecting anything but a little fun was a mistake. But he was exactly what she needed right now. In the midst of preparation for the Christmas Eve performance and having to deal with her family, Dante was a distraction. One any girl could appreciate.

Six

DANTE WALKED INTO the Fool's Gold fire station with a list and an idea for a plan. He spotted Charlie by her rig and called out to her.

She turned to him and raised her eyebrows. "You're wearing a suit."

He glanced down at his clothes and then back at her. "Yes."

"Looks uncomfortable."

"I'm used to it."

Charlie was tall, over five-ten, he would guess, with broad shoulders and plenty of muscle. He didn't know much about what it took to be a firefighter, but he knew physical strength was a part of it. Still, at that moment, she had the happy, glowing smile of a woman in love.

"You didn't come here to model clothes," she said. "What's up?"

"I heard you spoke to Evie about a work party

for her sets. I wanted to talk to you about that. How do I get something like that organized?"

"You volunteering?"

"I am."

"Know which end of a hammer hits the nail?"

"I've done construction."

She looked him up and down. "I have my doubts."

"It's how I got through my fancy college."

"Was it fancy?"

"There were bows and lace."

She grinned. "Okay, I like a man who can take a little teasing. Now, about the work party. Do you know Patience McGraw?"

"No."

"She's a hair stylist, and her daughter is in Evie's class. Which means nothing to you. Okay, the point is she mentioned the work party, as well. So we've been coordinating. Let me get my notes."

She disappeared out a side door, then reappeared a minute later, carrying a piece of paper. There were a couple of dozen names and phone numbers on it.

"Evie has a supply list," Dante told her. "We put that together when we went to see the sets."

"Good. We're thinking next Saturday. It's early enough in the season that not everyone is busy." She waved the names and phone numbers. "How many people are you willing to call?"

"As many as you want."

"I like that. You have potential." She tore the paper in half and handed one of the pieces to him. "Oh, and make sure Rafe, Shane and Clay are there. I keep meaning to mention it, but I haven't yet and I'm working a double shift."

"I'll get them there."

Charlie glanced at the list, then back at him. "Why are you helping Evie?"

A seemingly simple question with a complicated answer. Because the more he learned about her past, the more he wanted to knock a few heads together. As he couldn't do that, making her current dance crisis better was the other option. Because she was dynamite in tights and he was a man who enjoyed a beautiful woman. But maybe, most honestly, because this time of year he always missed his mom and he knew that helping out Evie would make his mother proud.

"Christmas is my thing," he said instead.

"Why do I think there's more to that story?"

EVIE PUSHED THE play button on the CD player and waited for the familiar music to begin. She'd warmed up already, and her first class wasn't for an hour. While there was plenty of paperwork to do and she still had to decide on the last transition in the show, she was restless. Her muscles nearly twitched, and her brain was fuzzy. She knew the solution. The question was, would her body co-operate?

She banged the box of her toe shoes against the floor a couple of times to make sure she'd tied them on correctly. The music surrounded her as she raised her arm. She silently counted to eight in her head, then, as the familiar notes filled the studio, moved both her feet and arms.

She'd never performed the "Dance of the Sugar Plum Fairy," although she'd been an understudy twice. Now she kept time with the music, landing in *effacé en fondu.* Her body wobbled slightly, but she kept on. *Revelé* and *passé.* Up. With ballet, the dancer was always lifting. In modern dance, she would go down first, as if scooping from the earth before going up, but in ballet, the goal was the sky. A turn and—

Pain ripped through her leg and her hip. Ignoring the fiery sensation, she raised herself again, her pelvis tucked, her body a perfect line from her head to her toes. Arms extended, her fingers curved delicately. The music guided her, the count pulsing in rhythm with her heartbeat.

She risked a glance in the mirror and immediately saw everything that was wrong. The sloppy extension, the bend of her elbow, the slight tilt. Voices echoed in her head. Calls for more crisp footwork, faster beats. Precision, perfection. The room seemed to bend and fade as time shifted.

She was seventeen again and walking into class at Juilliard.

The dance continued, and when the last note was silent, she came down on her feet and walked to the remote to start it again.

By the third time through, her leotard was damp with sweat. By the fifth, every muscle trembled and the fire in her leg had become a volcano of pain. She was both here and in her past. Remembering how eager she'd been, how full of dreams. How six months into her first year at the prestigious dance school she'd been told she didn't have what it took. Yes, she worked hard, was disciplined and determined. But she lacked the raw talent. The best she could hope for was the corps, with a second-rate company. They offered her the chance to leave rather than to be thrown out. A testament to their affection for her.

Evie's right leg gave way. Still-recovering muscles had reached the point of exhaustion, and she went down hard on the wood floor. She lay there, panting, shivering. After a few minutes she sat up and untied her shoes, then tossed them across the room and rested her head against her knees.

There were no tears. Nothing to cry for. She couldn't complain about what had been lost. Not when she'd never had it in the first place. Slowly the pain became manageable. She forced herself to her feet and limped over to the CD player to silence it before heading to the small restroom in the back of the studio.

She washed her face and made sure the braids around her head were still secure. She could see the sadness in her eyes, the lingering shadows of the pain, but doubted anyone else would notice. Her girls were excited about the performance. They all wanted to do their best.

She remembered what it was like to feel that way—back before she'd known that those kinds of dreams were impossible to hold on to. But maybe one of her students would have what it took. Maybe one of them would make it onto the stage and dance with a major company. They were on a journey, and she wanted to offer whatever guidance she could.

"I DON'T WORK for you."

Shane made the statement from his place on the sofa in Rafe's ranch house living room.

Dante nodded. "I'm glad you recognize that."

"Technically I don't work *for* him," Rafe pointed out. "I work with him."

"I'm with Shane," Clay said. He was sprawled in the big recliner with the best view of the big screen. Not that the TV was on. "So I don't come to your meetings."

"All evidence to the contrary," Dante told him.

It was shortly after noon on Tuesday. Rafe had

been working from home. As Shane's horses were on his property next to his brother's, getting him over to Rafe's house had been easy enough. Clay had texted he was available, as well, so here they all were.

"This Saturday is a work party. Charlie and Patience are setting it up."

"Patience?" Rafe asked. "Do I know her?"

"She's a hair stylist," Clay said. "Friends with Charlie, Heidi and Annabelle. You've met her."

"I don't think so," Rafe said, then glanced back at Dante. "But, okay. What does Patience have to do with anything?"

Dante groaned. "The point is the work party."

"What's it for?" Shane asked.

"Your sister."

The three brothers stared at him blankly.

"I thought she was renting her townhouse," Clay said. "What does she need help with?"

"The sets," Dante told them.

"Sets of what?" Rafe asked.

Dante had unexpected empathy for the women in his life who, from time to time, had stared at him like he was the stupidest man on earth.

"The sets for the dance."

Shane frowned. "Evie's going to a school dance?"

"*The Dance of the Winter King,* you morons. Your sister teaches dance. There's a performance on Christmas Eve. The manager of the school took off, leaving Evie in charge of everything. This is a big deal to the town, and she has to make it happen. The sets for the production are in bad shape. There's going to be a work party to refurbish them, and you will all be there to help."

The brothers looked at each other and then back at Dante.

"Sure," Shane said. "Why didn't you just say so?"

Dante sank into the chair behind him and rested his head in his hands. "It's too early for a beer, right?"

Rafe chuckled. "Don't sweat it. Of course we'll be there. When is it?"

"Saturday." Dante told them where to be. "Bring tools and paintbrushes." He raised his head. "Let me be clear. There won't be any excuses and you will be on time. You'll work hard, be cooperative and not do anything to upset your sister. Oh, and while I have you here, this is where I tell you that you will also be attending the performance. Got it?"

"Of course we'll be there," Rafe said, shifting in his seat. "We, ah, were always going to come."

"Right." Dante scowled at him. "You're a crappy liar."

"I know, but that makes me a good business

partner." Rafe drew in a breath. "Thanks for looking out for her."

"You're welcome."

THE FIFTEEN OR SO GIRLS were crowded around Evie's laptop, watching the DVD of the performance from three years ago.

"This is the part I was talking about," Evie said. "Until that last four-count, the dance is beautiful. See how everyone moves together? Then it comes to an end and there are three beats of nothing, followed by everyone clomping off the stage."

Melissa Sutton turned to Evie. "Do you really think they clomped?"

"I'm sure not in their hearts, but that's what it looks like." She walked away from the group, exaggerating her steps so she sounded more like an elephant than a dancer.

The girls all laughed.

"So we need something different," Evie said. "Something more lyrical."

Fifteen pairs of eyes watched her anxiously, both excited and a little nervous.

Her other classes were divided by age, skill level and style of dance. She had the six-year-olds who were awkward but adorable. The beginning class in tap and ballet for seven- to eleven-year-olds was popular. She taught one clog dancing class, several in modern dance. There were classes for those near-teens, who had several years of experience, and finally a ballet class for one group of serious students. Then there was this group—fifteen girls of all ages and abilities who were new to dance.

Melissa Sutton was the oldest, at fifteen. Her younger sister, Abby, was also in the class. The rest were around twelve or thirteen. The girls were tall, short and everything in between. A few were here because they had weight problems, and their pediatrician had suggested dance as a way to get exercise. None of them had any experience, and most lacked a sense of rhythm. But they were fun and enthused and Evie enjoyed teaching them. They were already nervous about the performance, and she wasn't looking to increase their anxiety.

"I thought we would try something simple. Who here has seen *Swan Lake?*"

A few of the girls raised their hands.

Evie walked over to her computer and changed the DVDs. "There's something called 'Pas de Quartre of the Small Swans.' It's four dancers together. I thought we could do something like that, but in groups of five."

She found the right part of the ballet and pushed the play button. The girls gathered around her computer. As the dance began, their eyes widened, and they all turned to stare at her.

"We can't do that," Melissa said. "We don't

know ballet. This is modern dance. And to go up on our toes like that?"

One of the bigger girls bit her lower lip. "I'd look stupid trying."

"No," Evie said quickly. "I'm not asking you to dance *en pointe*. I'm showing you the style of what I'm thinking we'll do for our exit."

She moved to the center of the room. "At the end of your dance, you're all in a row. Bent over like this." She counted the beats, then straightened and moved her arms.

"Now pretend I'm at the end of the row. We'll do three groups of five dancers, so I would go forward three counts." She motioned for Melissa to join her. "Stand here, with your arms crossed."

Melissa took Evie's left hand with her right.

"Good. Now quick steps to the right, on the balls of your feet, and one and two and three and four, straight, lifting."

Melissa did as she said, and they moved across the floor. Evie released her. She bent forward, her arms still crossed in front of her, then straightened and moved four more steps.

"I haven't gone to the stage yet, to do the actual count. I'm thinking it will be three combinations. As the first row moves to the right, the second row will move forward and follow."

Melissa nodded slowly. "I get it. It's the spirit of that bit from *Swan Lake,* without the scary parts."

Evie laughed. "Exactly. Want to do it with me?"

"Sure."

Evie put the music in the CD player. "We'll start from the beginning."

"One and two and three and four."

Evie and Melissa moved together in the simple dance. Her leg was still sore from her workout the previous day, but she was used to working through the pain. As they finished the three-minute routine, she reached for Melissa's hand and stepped to the side. The girl kept up, only stumbling twice.

"And we're off the stage," she said. "Easy enough?"

Her class glanced at each other, then back at her. Abby, Melissa's sister, nodded.

"I can do that."

"Me, too," one of the other girls said.

"I knew you could," Evie told them. "Now everyone line up, and we'll take it from the top."

It took the rest of class, but by the end all the girls were comfortable with the transition. As her students walked out of the studio, Evie went to turn off the CD. Melissa followed her.

"You're really patient with us," the teen said.

"You're great to work with."

"I know we're not as good as some of the other classes. I've seen Grace dance. She's amazing."

Grace was fourteen and one of the school's most promising students. Starting in January, Evie would be working with her privately. While each of the performers would get a chance to shine at the show, Grace had one of the only two longer solos.

"She's been studying since she was four," Evie told Melissa. "That's a long time."

"I know. I really like coming here, though."

"I'm glad. I hope you continue to dance."

Melissa wrinkled her nose. "Could I ever dance on my toes?"

"Of course. It's not that hard."

"Does it hurt?"

"Yes," Evie said with a laugh. "But you get used to it."

Melissa grinned. "I can't wait." She hugged Evie, then ran out.

Evie followed her toward the reception area and was surprised to find Dante there. Several of the mothers were helping their daughters into winter coats and boots, although Evie noticed more than a few of the moms were glancing toward the handsome attorney.

She couldn't blame them. The man dazzled in a suit. She had a feeling he would look just as good without one.

She watched her students leave, then turned to him.

"There's no clog dancing tonight," she said. "You have no reason to complain."

His blue eyes were dark with an emotion she couldn't read. He looked at the door, then back at her.

"Last class of the night?" he asked.

She nodded. "Everything will be quiet. Do you have to phone Shanghai again?"

"Not exactly."

He took a step toward her, then put his hands on her waist and drew her against him. She went easily, wanting to feel his arms around her. She was overwhelmed by all she had to accomplish before the performance, a little freaked out by the holiday season and uncomfortable about having her family so close. The idea of forgetting all that in a passionate embrace suddenly seemed like a great idea.

He lowered his mouth to hers. She tilted her head, let her eyes close and her hands settle on his broad shoulders. Then she gave herself over to the soft, warm insistence of Dante's kiss.

Seven

DANTE TASTED OF mint and warmth. His mouth moved against hers, back and forth, exploring, teasing. She found herself wanting more from him, so she tightened her hold on his shoulders and leaned in slightly.

Her body came in contact with his. He was all hard muscles. She felt delicate next to him—feminine. His hands spanned her back, his fingers pressing lightly against her. The leotard didn't offer much in the way of a barrier, and he quickly heated her.

She kissed him back, moving her mouth as well, then parted her lips. He slipped inside, his tongue lightly stroking hers. She went up on tiptoe and wrapped her arms around his neck, even as they kissed more deeply.

Low in her belly, wanting blossomed. Her thighs ached for a reason that had nothing to do with exercise and everything to do with anticipation. Her blood moved more quickly, spreading desire to every part of her.

He drew back enough to stare into her eyes. "You're dangerous."

She smiled. "Hardly."

"Sexy, tempting and the whole dance thing. I'm getting all these images in my head."

"Imagining what I can do?" she asked.

"Oh, yeah."

Dante was one of those men who liked to be in control, she thought. It came with his profession and partially from his personality. She would guess he nearly always had the upper hand in his relationships.

Still on tiptoe, she leaned in to whisper in his ear. "Whatever you're thinking, I can do more."

She slowly lowered herself until she was standing flat-footed. Dante's eyes were glazed, his mouth slightly parted. The comment was mostly cheap talk. Sure, she was limber and strong and could probably get in positions that he'd only dreamed about, but so what? That didn't mean she was any more secure than other women. She still worried about how she looked naked and whether or not the relationship would have a happy ending.

He shook his head, as if clearing his mind, then swore under his breath. "It's the dancing," he muttered. "You're too sexy."

"Thank you, but the truth is, I'm not that good a dancer."

"You're the best I've ever seen."

She laughed. "Again, a lovely compliment, but you're hardly a discriminating audience." She thought about the feel of his mouth on hers. "Good kisses, though."

"You like them?"

"I do."

"Good. Then we should plan to kiss more."

A goal she could get behind. Dante might not be long-term material, but didn't she deserve a little fun? It was the holiday season. He could be her gift to herself. Being with him was easy and natural. She needed more of that in her life.

He cleared his throat and deliberately put space between them. "Okay, there's a reason I came to talk to you."

"Which is?"

"The work party is arranged. Charlie and Patience have taken care of most of the volunteers. I'm picking up the supplies tomorrow. We're starting at eight on Saturday morning."

"At the warehouse?"

He nodded. "We have a big workspace. If everyone who says he's coming does, we're going to need it." He paused. "Your brothers will be there."

She looked at him. "Your doing?"

"Maybe."

She wanted to say she didn't need them, that she would be fine on her own. But the truth was, she didn't know anything about refurbishing sets for a production. She needed help, and she would be grateful for anyone who showed up.

"Thank you," she told him.

"You mean that?"

"Nearly."

He laughed and kissed her lightly on the mouth. "Close enough. I gotta go. See you Saturday?"

"I'm looking forward to it."

"Me, too."

EVIE MANAGED TO hang on to the post-kiss tingles during her walk home. A trick, considering the temperature had to be close to freezing. There were plenty of stars in the sky, but the next storm would bring snow to Fool's Gold.

Still, despite the occasional shiver, she felt warm inside. Or maybe just quivery. There was something about a man who knew how to kiss. No doubt Dante had plenty of practice with the women in his life. Something she should remember to keep herself safe. In the meantime, she would enjoy the anticipation. •

As she turned onto her street, she noticed there were more decorations on the various houses and townhomes. Lights on roof lines, and plastic snow-men and Santas on lawns. By contrast, Dante's place was completely dark and hers only had a few flameless candles in the front windows. Maybe she should find out about getting some lights for the front window and maybe a wreath for her door.

As she walked up to the porch, she glanced next door. Obviously Dante wasn't home yet. She wondered how late he was going to work and wished they had the kind of relationship where she could simply call and invite him over for dinner. Not that she had anything to eat. Still, they could get takeout. Maybe Chinese.

She went inside and flipped on lights. After hanging up her jacket, she hit the switch for the gas fireplace, then waited for the *whoosh* as it started up. She wandered into the kitchen, already knowing there was nothing to eat, and wondered why ordering takeout for one didn't sound as exciting as when it was for two.

Someone rang her doorbell.

Evie felt herself starting to smile as she hurried back to the living room. Dante was home, she thought happily. He'd decided to come over and—

She pulled open the door, then felt her whole body tense as she stared at her mother.

"Hello, Evie," May said.

"Mom." She automatically stepped back to allow the other woman in, then wished she hadn't.

"How are you?" May asked.

"Fine. I just got home from work."

"The girls are getting ready for their performance?"

Evie nodded, then watched as her mother slipped off her coat and hung it on the back of a chair.

The Stryker brothers all shared similar looks. Dark hair and eyes they'd inherited from both their parents. The brothers were tall, with broad shoulders and muscles. Evie assumed she took after her father—not only with her light coloring, but with her lean build. When the family was together, no one questioned who the brothers belonged to. Strangers had always assumed Evie was someone else's child. As she'd gotten older, she'd been presumed to be the girlfriend or a neighbor.

"I thought we could talk," May said, sitting on the sofa and patting the cushion next to her.

Evie tried to figure out a way to say she was too busy, but she couldn't come up with an excuse. And knowing May, her mother would want to know what was more important than them talking.

"All right."

Evie sat in a chair across from her mother, rather than next to her, and waited.

May looked around. "You don't have a lot of furniture."

"The place came furnished."

May nodded. "That's right. Your apartment in Los Angeles was furnished, too."

"I like to travel light."

"Eventually you'll want to settle down." Her mother looked at her. "I was hoping you'd stay at the ranch a little longer. It was nice having you there."

Evie drew in a breath. "With me working in town, this is more convenient." She hoped she would get points for being polite because what she really wanted to say was "Why on earth would I want to live anywhere near you?" But that sounded harsh, even in her own mind.

It wasn't fair—her mother had been horrible to her for years and years. But Evie was now expected to be reasonable. To understand, maybe even forgive. When was it her turn to be the mean one? Not that she wanted to be mean, but she wanted some kind of payback.

No, that wasn't right, she thought, shifting on the chair. She honestly wasn't sure what she wanted, but it wasn't them pretending all was well.

May drew in a breath. "Fool's Gold has many holiday traditions. Even more than I remember from when we lived here before. On the fifteenth is the annual Day of Giving. The town welcomes all kinds of charities to come in and talk about what they do. There are booths set up, and people can ask questions. The same day is the Take Home a Pet Adoption."

Evie wasn't sure where this was going. Money

was always tight in her world, and right now she was saving every extra penny she had. Not that there were very many of them.

"Carina McKenzie started the pet adoption last year, but she's pregnant now and can't be on her feet that much. Rina, as everyone calls her, is married to Cameron McKenzie."

May paused expectantly.

Evie shrugged. "Okay," she said cautiously. "Should I know who that is?"

May smiled. "Right. Sorry. You have no reason to. Cameron is our local vet."

Evie thought about all the animals on the ranch. There was everything from goats to horses and even Priscilla, an aging Indian elephant.

"You must want to keep him happy," she said.

May laughed. "Exactly. So when Rina started to freak out about the pet adoption, I told her I would help. I thought it was something we could do together."

At first Evie thought her mother meant "together," as in "with Rina." It took her a second to process the hopeful stare and realize May wanted her only daughter to help.

"I know, I know," her mother said quickly. "You're very busy with the dance. I understand that. Rina is going to arrange all the advertising and get the word out about the adoption. I'm handling the pet end. Going to see the animals at the shelter, arranging for grooming, setting up for the event and handling the actual adoptions. It's only one Saturday. We could have fun."

May paused, her expression hopeful.

Evie opened her mouth, then closed it. Everything about the situation was unfair, she thought with mild annoyance. If she said no, she was the bad guy. If she said yes, she would get stuck doing something she didn't want to do.

"It wouldn't be much time," her mother added.

Evie drew in a breath. "Sure," she said slowly, knowing if she didn't agree, the guilt would keep her awake that night.

May beamed at her. "Wonderful. I'll handle all the details, I promise. We only have a couple of weeks until the adoption and I want it to go well."

May bounced to her feet. Evie instinctively stood as well, then found herself pulled into her mother's embrace. They stood there for a second, hugging. Evie couldn't remember the last time that had happened, but she told herself to simply relax and accept the gesture in the spirit in which it was meant.

For a second, she allowed herself to feel the longing she'd lived with as a kid. Shut out of her family, always the outsider. Never fitting in or knowing how to belong. Back then, having her mom hug her would have meant the world. Now it was simply awkward.

She thought about what Dante had told her—
that now some of the responsibility was hers. That
if she wanted things to be better, she was going to
have to be a part of the solution. But as she stood
there, uncomfortable and unsure, she realized she
didn't have a clue as to how to change anything.
Nor did she know if she was really willing to risk
her heart one more time.

Eight

EVIE WAS DRESSED and hovering by the front door fifteen minutes before Dante was due to arrive. It was barely seven and well below freezing. But the skies were clear, so there still wasn't any snow.

This morning was the work party for her sets and she was nervous about everything getting done. While the sets were simple and the dancers the focus of the performances, the backdrops provided context and mood. No one would expect perfection from an amateur show, but she was determined to get as close to professional as possible.

She opened the front door when she saw him walking up the front steps. He smiled when he saw her.

"You look nervous," he said.

"What if we don't get everything done? I'm trying not to freak out, and it's difficult."

He leaned in and kissed her cheek. "Have a little faith."

"I have great faith in you," she told him. "It's myself and everyone else who causes me doubt. I've barely held a paintbrush."

"Now you'll be able to practice."

She grabbed her jacket and followed him outside. Instead of his sleek German import, a large pickup truck was parked in his driveway.

"Compliments of your sister-in-law," he said.

She slid onto the seat and stared at him. "You borrowed Heidi's truck?"

He shrugged. "I knew if I asked one of your brothers to trade with me, he would probably drive my car. Heidi won't."

She grinned. "Are you sure about that? She has a bit of a wild streak. What if she takes one of her goats for a joyride?"

"Now you're just messing with me. Come on. We need to get our supplies and be at the warehouse before our workers show up."

Ten minutes later Dante was backing toward the loading dock of the Fool's Gold hardware store. Two teenagers were ready with stacks of paint, brushes, tarps, glue and bags filled with Evie wasn't sure what. Dante went over his master list, and Evie signed the purchase order. The store would bill Dominique, the dance studio's owner, directly.

By quarter to eight, they'd stopped for coffee and were on their way to the warehouse. Evie told herself that whatever work they got done would be enough and that she shouldn't be disappointed if no one showed up to help. People had busy lives, and it wasn't as if she had a bunch of friends in town. Sure, Charlie and Patience had offered to make a few calls, but would that make a difference? Patience would be there, Evie knew, but Charlie had to work at the fire station. Still, with one or two parents and her brothers, they could make some serious progress.

Dante pulled into the storage warehouse parking lot. She saw there were already about ten or fifteen cars and trucks there.

As she climbed out of the truck, Patience hurried toward her, her long brown hair pulled back in a ponytail.

"'Morning," she said cheerfully. "I'm just organizing the work parties now. The sets have already been pulled out and grouped together by scene. I was waiting to hear what you think about how we're going to do this."

Not sure she would have an opinion, Evie followed her inside the large building.

Instead of the sets being stacked together in the cramped storage locker, they were spread out in the long, open hallway of the warehouse. Sure enough, they had been clustered together by scene and in chronological order. She could look at them and see the flow of the show.

More surprising was the setup. Long tables stood at one end. Heaters were plugged in the whole length of the hall. Lights blazed overhead. But the most amazing part of all was the people waiting. There had to be at least twenty adults and several of her dance students. As Evie blinked in astonishment, two more families arrived, including Melissa and Abby Sutton. They were accompanied by a boy, who was probably their brother, and their parents. Rafe, Shane and Clay were also there, smiling at her with an annoying combination of pride and smugness.

"Surprised?" Clay asked.

"Yes," she admitted.

"Good. We decided you needed more surprises in your life."

"Lucky me."

"By eight-thirty we won't be able to move in here," Patience told her. "But, hey, the more hands, the better, right? This way, we'll get it all done by noon."

Evie opened her mouth, then closed it. Her throat was tight, and she had the horrifying thought that she might actually start to cry. She'd been hoping for a couple of parents to show up. Not a flood of assistance from people she didn't even know.

"I, um," she began, then waved her arms, not sure what to say.

Dante took one of her hands in his and squeezed her fingers. "I'm the professional here," he told her. "Why don't you let me organize everyone into groups? You can supervise."

"Thank you," she said, vowing to bake him a cake or something later. Okay, maybe baking wasn't the best way to show her appreciation, but she would come up with a plan.

"Stryker brothers," he called. "Come with me to unload the truck. Everyone else, pick a set and go stand by it. Make sure you divide yourselves evenly."

Five other guys went with Dante and her brothers. By the time they'd returned, there were at least twenty more people there to help. The hallway was loud and crowded. While a few people had collected by sets, most were just laughing and talking. They'd moved from controlled chaos to a party.

"How do you want to handle this?" Dante asked. He had a paint can in each hand.

Patience stood with her clipboard but didn't look as if she was going to take charge. Evie knew she was ultimately responsible for the project. What was that old saying? An embarrassment of riches. She needed to get over it, she told herself.

She walked over to a folding chair and climbed onto the seat. Her injured leg protested slightly, but she ignored the twinge and waited as people turned toward her and grew quiet.

Everyone was staring at her, she thought, feeling herself flush. She knew less than a third of the adults in the room. The only time she'd ever been anything close to a leader was while she was teaching. Still, the performance was her responsibility, and that made the sets her problem.

"I'd like to thank everyone for taking time out of your Saturday to come here and help. I know the holidays are especially busy, so your generosity is all the more appreciated. For those of you who arrived in the past fifteen minutes, we're asking everyone to gather around the set you want to work on."

She pointed to the chronological beginning of the story. "I'll walk down the line and tell you what I would like done. The supplies will be on those tables at the end. We may have to share cans of paint and brushes."

"I brought tools," a man called. "Three toolboxes, nails, screws, extra lumber."

"Thank you." Evie smiled at the crowd. "You're all fantastic for coming out here today. I hope you'll enjoy our performance."

"We always love the show," a woman said.

Everyone applauded and Evie stepped down.

She walked over to the first set. Patience walked with her.

"I'll take notes," the other woman said. "So we can keep track of what's going to be done."

"Thank you."

One of the men standing by the first set, a good-looking blond guy with an easy smile, pointed to the back of the tall trees.

"The supports are all busted," he said. "We should replace them while we're painting. It won't take long and Ethan is here to give us novices advice."

Evie cleared her throat. "Ethan?"

"The guy who said he had tools."

A pretty, obviously pregnant woman with brown hair joined the man. "Josh, start with the basics." She smiled at Evie. "I'm Charity Golden. This is my husband, Josh. Ethan Hendrix is a local contractor."

"Thanks for coming."

"Oh, we love helping out. This is a fun project. Our daughter is still too tiny to be involved in anything, so we're practicing for when she's older."

Josh leaned over and patted his wife's tummy. "And he."

Charity rolled her eyes. "Yes, this one is a boy and Josh is too proud for words." But there was love in her voice as she spoke, and the couple shared a look that spoke of devotion and caring.

Evie went over the rest of the repairs and agreed that, yes, this was a good time to deal with the trees.

She and Patience went down the line. Her brothers and Dante had claimed the throne where the Winter King sat. She looked at the four of them. "Tell me you know what you're doing."

Clay pressed a hand to his chest. "Mortal blow. Come on, sis, we're good. Dante and Rafe have both done construction, and Shane and I will follow their instructions."

She sighed. "Fine, but no fighting."

By eight-thirty, everyone was hard at work. She walked up and down the line, pleased with how quickly things were progressing. Close to nine, a tall, dark-haired man walked into the warehouse. He had as many muscles as Wolverine and looked nearly as dangerous. He glanced around at everyone working, caught sight of Evie and headed directly for her.

"I'm Gideon," he told her, his low voice rubbing against her skin like velvet. Or maybe chocolate.

"Okay," she said, wanting to get him to speak again. A voice like that was magic. "I'm Evie."

His dark eyes glinted with amusement but his mouth didn't smile. "I own both radio stations here in town."

"That's nice."

Patience cleared her throat and leaned close. "He's, ah, doing the narration for the performance."

Evie looked back at him. "Oh. Gideon. We've emailed." Had she known what his voice sounded like, she would have asked that they speak on the phone instead of meeting in person. "Nice to meet you."

They shook hands.

"I've watched the performances on DVD," he said. "And I went over the script. I thought about making a few changes." He handed her several sheets of paper. "To smooth things out and make the story flow better."

"Sure. I'm open to that." She took the papers he offered.

He was a good-looking guy with a seductive voice. She was currently unattached, although secretly attracted to her neighbor. Shouldn't Gideon be getting her tingles on? After all, she could simply close her eyes and listen to the magic of him speaking.

She glanced at the script, all the while trying to imagine sharing dinner with the smooth-talking stranger. But instead of enjoying the visual, her brain replaced Gideon with Dante and then got all quivery. So much for the magic voice working on her sexually. Apparently she simply enjoyed it the way she enjoyed good music or a latte. At least now she didn't have to find out if he was single.

She smiled at him. "There are too many distractions for me to read this now. Can I get back to you?"

"Sure." He glanced around. "You've got quite the party here."

"I know. Patience and Charlie put out word that I needed help and look what happened." She lowered her voice. "I'm not from here, so it's kind of a surprise."

"I know what you mean. I've only been in town for about two months and it's not like anywhere else I've lived."

"Big-city guy?" she asked.

He shrugged. "That works as well as any other description. I'm retired military, so I've been all over the world."

"How did you find Fool's Gold?"

"A buddy told me about it. I came for a weekend and ended up buying the radio stations."

Melissa hurried over. "We're putting on the glitter. Can you come tell us if it's okay?"

"Sure." Evie smiled at Gideon. "Nice to finally meet you."

"You, too."

She followed Melissa over to one of the sets. When she turned back, Gideon was gone.

Work continued. Just before ten, Morgan, the owner of Morgan's Books and the man who played the famous Winter King, showed up with coffee and cupcakes for everyone. Evie introduced herself to the older man.

"I like what you're doing," he told her, his

brown eyes kind as he spoke. "A few of the girls have stopped by to tell me about the changes you're making in the show. They're very excited."

"I hope everyone enjoys the performance."

"They will." He nodded toward the throne. "The fur is a nice touch."

"Fur?" She followed his gaze and saw her brothers had attached faux snow-leopard fur trim to the throne. "Excuse me," she said to Morgan, then hurried the length of the hall.

"Fur?" she demanded when she reached the throne. "Are you serious?"

"Annabelle thought it would look nice," Shane said, his tone warning. "She gave it to me and I put it on."

"Fine." Evie liked her sister-in-law to-be and wasn't about to take on Shane over fur. "Any other surprises?"

"If we told you, they wouldn't be surprises," Clay said.

"Great."

Patience appeared at her side, clipboard in hand. "We're making great progress. With everyone drinking coffee and eating cupcakes, we should get a nice rush in productivity and have all the work done in another hour or so."

This time yesterday Evie would have said there was no way the sets could be spruced up in less than four hours. But now, surrounded by thirty or forty people digging in and getting it done, she realized it was more than possible.

"Thank you," Evie told her. "This wouldn't have happened without you and Charlie helping me."

"You're wonderful with Lillie, so I figure we're even. Oh, I forgot to tell you, we're all confirmed for the costumes and the makeup and hair. You know that's all provided, right? We have a fitting and make sure the girls are set with the clothes, then talk about hair and makeup."

The throat tightness was back again as she remembered the feuding stylist sisters story. "Let me guess. A couple of the local salons team up to take care of hair and makeup?"

"Exactly."

"Is this place even real?"

"Of course it is. I know it seems like we're really nice, but the truth is we're pretty nosy, and getting involved means we get the good gossip first."

Evie laughed. "I think the motivations are more altruistic than that."

"Which means we have you fooled." Patience started to say something else, but despite her open mouth, she was silent.

"What?" Evie asked, turning to follow her gaze. All she saw was some older woman with white hair walking into the warehouse. "You know her?"

"That's Mayor Marsha," Patience said, her voice hushed.

"Okay. Is it bad she's here?"

"No. She always comes to things like this. It's just…" Patience pointed. "Look."

Evie did and saw nothing out of the ordinary. "You've got to give me a clue."

"Look at what she's wearing!"

"Jeans and a cardigan over a turtleneck?"

"She's in *pants*."

"Uh-huh. You know women have been wearing pants out in public for maybe a hundred years."

"Not Mayor Marsha. She always wears a suit with a skirt. OMG."

Evie started to laugh. "You did not just say OMG."

"It's Mayor Marsha in jeans. It's an OMG moment. I have to go call my mom. She'll die when I tell her."

Patience pulled her cell phone out of her jacket pocket and pushed a button. Evie shook her head and walked back toward the people working.

Over the next hour, each of the sets was completed. Evie thanked the teams as they finished. She introduced herself to the mayor, who was a very pleasant woman. From what Evie could tell, no one else had shared Patience's reaction to the mayor wearing pants.

"Thank you," Evie told a blonde woman and her husband. "I'm sorry, I know you said your name, but I..." The woman was one of the triplets, but Evie had no idea which one.

"Don't worry. You've met way too many people today. You can't keep us all straight. I'm Nevada Janack and this is my husband, Tucker."

Evie shook hands with both of them, telling herself Nevada was pregnant. That information would help her keep the name with the face, at least until Nevada gave birth. "You were both wonderful. You didn't need to rebuild that whole section."

"It needed it," Tucker said. "Not to worry. Nevada and I are both in construction. So's Will." He pointed to the man who had been assisting them.

The three of them had taken apart the last set and basically created a new version from scratch. Now it was painted, and the pulley system for the falling snow gleamed with new hardware.

"Good luck with the show," Tucker said, then turned to his wife. "I'm going to help Will load the truck."

"Sure," Nevada said, then she looked at Evie. "My two sisters said to say they're sorry they couldn't make it. They both have kids on the tail end of colds."

"That's fine. We had plenty of people."

Nevada leaned toward her and lowered her voice. "Be grateful they didn't come. One of my brothers is in the military. He just told us he's not reenlisting, which means he's coming home next year."

Evie wasn't sure what that had to do with her sets. "Okay. You must all be happy."

"We are. We haven't spent any time with Ford in years. But the thing is, my sisters are determined to get him married off as quickly as possible. They're making a list of potential women and you're on it."

"Oh." Evie took a step back. "While I'm flattered, I, ah…"

"Can get your own guy? That's what I told them. Not that they'll listen. Ford's great. Don't get me wrong, but matchmaking is a slick road to disaster."

"I appreciate the warning."

"Anytime."

Technically, it wouldn't ever be an issue, Evie thought. She wasn't planning to be here a year from now. Although it made her kind of sad to think she wouldn't be working on the dance again.

Nevada, Tucker and Will gathered their tools and left. Evie's brothers had finished with the throne and were now checking to see which sets were dry and ready to be put away.

The nearly empty hallway smelled of paint and glue. The coffee and cupcakes had disappeared, and sometime when she hadn't been looking, someone had cleaned up the brushes and neatly stacked the cans of paint.

Shane and Rafe wheeled the throne back into the storage locker while Clay crossed to Evie.

"Five of the sets need to dry a little more before we store them," he told her. "I talked to the manager, and he said we can leave the sets out as long as they're not in the way. I'll swing by later and put them back into storage."

"I can do it," she said, surprised he would offer.

"Some of them are heavy. I'll take care of it." He draped his arm over her shoulder. "Then you'll owe me and I like the sound of that."

"Thanks," she told him.

"No problem."

Clay joined his brothers. A few minutes later, Dante and Evie were left alone in the warehouse. She pulled out her phone and glanced at the time.

"It's not even noon."

"Told you," Dante said. "You have to have a little faith in people."

"Oh, please. You're a lawyer. Faith is hardly your strong suit."

"I have my moments." He tucked a strand of hair behind her ear. "The tree lighting ceremony is tonight. Want to go with me?"

The sense of anticipation that had been so obviously quiet when she'd been speaking to Gideon fluttered to life in her tummy. She felt herself smil-

ing up at Dante and hoped she didn't look as fool-
ish as she felt.

"I'd like that."

"Pick you up at six. We'll eat on the way."

Nine

"YOU WERE RIGHT," Evie said, sipping the tea Charlie had made for them.

Charlie sat across from her in the kitchen at the fire station and smiled. "That never gets old. Maybe you could say it again."

Evie laughed. "I'm happy to. You were right. People showed up to help me with the sets. Lots of people. I didn't know most of them and yet there they were. Everything was done by noon. I never expected anything like that to happen. And yes, I know. I need to have faith in people. I've been told."

"Then my work here is done." Charlie leaned back in her chair.

"I met Gideon."

"What's he like? I've heard him on the radio. Sexy voice."

"Tell me about it. He's attractive, in a dangerous sort of way."

"That should make him irresistible." Charlie arched her eyebrows. "Any interest?" She held up a hand. "Never mind. I apologize for asking. I can't believe I'm turning into one of those women who falls in love and then wants to see everyone around her paired up, as well. It's horrible."

"I don't mind. And sorry, no. Gideon seemed very nice, but there was no chemistry." She wasn't about to mention her attraction to Dante. The fewer people who knew about that, the better.

"I'm glad the town came through for you," Charlie told her. "This place is always special, but even more so at the holidays." She hesitated. "Now I'm going to say something else I'll have to apologize for, but I can't help myself."

Evie held on to her mug and waited.

"It's your mom," Charlie began.

Evie stiffened. "What about her?"

"It's not my business," she began.

"You're right, it's not."

Charlie sighed. "And I always hated when people gave me advice about my mother. She and I didn't get along, either. But last summer she showed up here and wanted us to be close. I won't go into the reasons, but I will say I resisted. Only she didn't go away and one day I realized she was the only family I had. That without her, I had no biological connection to another person on this planet. That was kind of sobering."

"I know you're trying to help," Evie said grudgingly.

"I would have bet you every penny I had that my mother would never change," Charlie told her. "But I was wrong. And if Dominique can do it, May is more than capable. Your mom cares about you."

"Now," Evie muttered. "But back when it mattered, she was never there for me."

Charlie leaned toward her. "That sucks. She was wrong and she needs to understand that. I just have one question. If she's genuinely sorry and regrets what she did, how is she supposed to make it okay now?"

"I don't understand."

"If she feels remorse and asks for your forgiveness, what will make you grant it? She can't undo the past. So how do you find closure? How do you move on?"

"I don't know," Evie admitted. "I don't think I want to forgive her."

"So you'll both always be in pain? That doesn't sound very pleasant. Are you sure you want to live that way?"

"No, I don't," Evie said before she could stop herself. "But why does she get a free pass?"

"Because in any other alternative, you have to pay, too. Aren't you tired of that?"

Evie nodded slowly. "I want normal," she admitted. "I want to have a family who cares about me and whom I can care about." She wanted so much more than she had.

"You either make it work with the family you have or go find a new one. I hate to break it to you, but you're kind of past the cute kid stage."

Evie managed a smile. "You think? Because I look adorable in a tutu."

She knew Charlie was right. May had acknowledged the past, which was a big step. She was also reaching out. But part of her wanted to stomp her foot and insist it was too little, too late.

Dante had pointed out that she had responsibility for the relationship as it existed today. That if she wanted things to be different, she had to make a little effort.

The past couldn't be fixed, but maybe there was a way for the hole inside of her to be healed. Was being a part of something worth the work it would take?

Just then alarms went off in the station.

"Gotta go," Charlie said as she jumped to her feet and ran toward the engine bay.

Evie stayed where she was until the ambulance and fire engine had left, then she started for home. Dante was picking her up in a few hours. Until then she was going to try on everything in her closet until she found the perfect thing to wear tonight.

As for the question of what to do with her family—that she would release into the universe. Maybe with a little time, the answer would present itself all on its own.

In the end, comfort and warmth won over fashion. Evie pulled on long underwear, which meant she wasn't going to fit into her skinniest jeans. She layered a camisole under a sweater, over which she would wear a jacket. As the tree lighting ceremony was going to involve a lot of standing around, cute boots that pinched her toes were out of the question. So much for being dazzling, she thought as she gave in completely and tossed a pair of mittens on the sofa.

She did take the time to use hot rollers, then finger comb her hair into a tangle of curls. She brushed on a second coat of mascara and then applied peppermint-flavored lip gloss in case there was mistletoe. She was ready five minutes before Dante was due to arrive.

Fortunately he was four minutes early. She opened the door and hoped she didn't look as excited as she felt. Maybe being cool was out of the question, but there was no excuse for acting as eager as a puppy.

"Hi," he said as he stepped inside. "You look great."

"Thanks. You, too."

He had on jeans and boots, a leather jacket and a scarf that made his dark blue eyes even sexier. He smelled of wood smoke and pine, and when he leaned in to kiss her, she felt herself melting.

His mouth claimed hers with a combination of hunger and tenderness. After the first brush of skin-on-skin, he drew back and raised his eyebrows.

"Peppermint?"

She shrugged. "It's seasonal."

"I like it."

He closed the front door, then cupped her cheeks in his large hands and lowered his mouth to hers. This time, instead of kissing her, he lightly licked her bottom lip. Tasting maybe, she thought, as wanting made her weak. She pressed her fingers against the cold leather of his jacket, wishing she could get a lot closer.

He waited until she parted for him, then swept his tongue inside. They strained toward each other, kissing more deeply, passion growing until she felt herself start to tremble.

This time she was the one to draw back, her breathing uneven, her head spinning. Spending time with Dante was great. She enjoyed his company, and she felt oddly safe around him. But taking things to the next level? She would have to make sure she kept a firm hold on her heart before she could let that happen. She deserved a little fun but didn't want to let that morph into anything more than that.

"I want to say it's the dance clothes," he murmured, staring into her eyes. "Only you're fully dressed. So it must be you."

She managed a smile. "You're saying I'm a temptation?"

"I'm saying you're on my mind a lot these days."

Words to make her quiver.

For a second she thought about suggesting they pass on the tree lighting ceremony. That her bedroom was only a short staircase away. Except, she needed to be sure she knew what she was doing.

"Don't worry," Dante said, lightly kissing the tip of her nose. "We have a date with a tree and you know how they get if we're late. All sad and then the pine needles fall off. We can't disappoint the children of Fool's Gold just because I find you the sexiest woman in three counties."

That made her laugh. She stepped back and grabbed her coat. "Only three? Who's the competition?"

"A former Miss Apple Valley, four counties away."

"I hate her already."

She zipped her coat. Dante tucked in her scarf, then handed her the mittens. He opened the front door and they stepped into the night.

"You're saying if Miss Apple Valley came calling, you'd dump me in a heartbeat?" she asked, tucking her hand around the crook of his elbow.

"It's a serious possibility."

"And here I was holding out for Matt Damon."

"A married man? I'm shocked and more than a little disappointed."

They were still laughing as they walked toward town.

The evening was clear and cold. Their breath came in white puffs of steam.

"I have a feeling I didn't layer enough," she said as they turned toward the center of town.

"I'll keep you warm," Dante promised.

They weren't the only ones out. The lighting of the town Christmas tree was a big deal, and the sidewalks were crowded. Most of the stores were open. Signs in the windows promised everything from hot chocolate to hot apple cider. There were stands selling homemade cookies and funnel cakes. Christmas music played from speakers.

"Evie, Dante! Good to see you!"

Evie heard someone calling their names but couldn't see who it was. She waved in the general direction of the voice.

"Any clue?" she asked Dante.

"Not even one."

"It's kind of scary that people know who we are."

"As long as they don't chase us with pitchforks."

There were more booths set up by the town square where the crowd was the thickest. Evie hung on to Dante, knowing if they weren't careful, they would get separated.

"Hey, you two." Evie turned and saw Charlie walking toward them. She was with a blonde woman carrying a toddler.

At first Evie wanted to say the woman was Nevada Janack, only the hair wasn't the same and there was something different about her smile. Plus she didn't look pregnant. Clay trailed along behind Charlie, his gaze locked firmly on his fiancée.

"Evie, this is Dakota Andersson. You met her sister Nevada this morning." Charlie leaned close. "You're not going crazy. They're triplets."

"Oh, right. I remember that from the brunch. It's good to see you again."

Dakota laughed. "You, too. My sister Montana is the one who's missing tonight. She's crushed not to be here, but her baby and mine both got a cold and are recovering. My mom is home with Jordan Taylor because we didn't want Hannah to miss tonight." She kissed her daughter's cheek. "Daddy is off getting us hot chocolate."

"It's nice to meet you," Evie said. "This is Dante Jefferson, my brother's business partner."

"Hi." Dakota nodded at him, then turned back to Evie. "I was wondering if there's a toddler class at the dance school. Hannah saw *The Nutcracker* on TV and can't stop talking about it. I know kids can start dance classes pretty young. I went online, but there isn't a website for the studio."

Evie considered the question. "The youngest students I have are six," she said slowly. "But you're right. A lot of girls start much younger than that."

A class for three- and four-year-olds could be during the day, which would be easier on her schedule. Maybe early afternoon. She could even consider a Mommy and Me type class. As for the performance, if the toddlers went first...

There was no point in thinking about that, she told herself. Her plan was to leave town long before next year's show. So the toddlers weren't her problem. But for a second, she thought about how adorable they would be as they danced.

"Let me get through the holiday show," she told Dakota. "If you want to give me a call after the first of the year, we can talk about starting a class for the younger kids. I would enjoy teaching them."

"Thank you. Have a great holiday. I'll be calling."

She walked off with Charlie. Clay paused to give Evie a brief hug before joining his fiancée.

"Can three-year-olds dance?" Dante asked, sounding doubtful.

"Sure. It's good for them to study dance as they're still developing. If done correctly, the practice will improve their motor skills, balance and posture. As long as the training isn't too rigorous or boring. At that age, dance should be fun."

"And when they're older?"

"If they're serious, then it's a lot of hard work." Talent was also required, she thought, remembering what it had been like when she'd been told she didn't have what it took to make it at Juilliard. It didn't matter that she'd trained the longest, had given the most. Without the raw ability, she would never be good enough.

They walked toward the square at the center of town. Light from the streetlamps reflected off the decorations, but until it was lit, the huge tree was little more than a hulking shadow in the darkness.

Evie recognized a few families in the crowd and waved at the people who had taken the time to help with her sets. She leaned into Dante.

"Thanks for talking to my brothers," she said. "For getting them to help."

"I didn't do much."

"You made sure they showed up. That was nice. Thank you."

He groaned. "Not nice. Don't say nice. I would rather be the hot, sexy lawyer you can't resist."

She grinned at him but thought privately that he was all that and more.

He looked at her. "They want to be there for you, Evie. You just have to give them a chance."

Before she could decide if she agreed or not, Shane and Annabelle wandered up and stood next to them. Annabelle was flushed from the cold and munching on a funnel cake.

"I'm eating for twenty," Annabelle announced. "That can't be good, right?"

"You're beautiful," Shane told her.

"I'm going to need my own zip code." Annabelle took another bite and chewed. When she'd swallowed, she looked at Evie. "I need you to be an elf."

Evie stared at her. "Excuse me?"

"Okay, technically it's not me. It's Heidi. Even not pregnant I wouldn't be a good elf. I'm too short."

Evie knew for a fact that Annabelle wasn't drinking, so she had no explanation for the confusing topic of conversation.

Shane put his arm around his fiancée. "You have to start at the beginning."

"What? Oh. The ranch offers holiday sleigh rides. We decorate the sleighs and the horses. Of course if there's no snow, then they're wagon rides. We have hot cocoa and cookies and…"

"Elves?" Dante offered helpfully.

Annabelle nodded.

"I have to get everyone ready for *The Dance of the Winter King,*" Evie said quickly, thinking she didn't have time to be an elf.

"It's only for a couple of evenings. Heidi will know for sure." Annabelle finished the last of the funnel cake, then looked hopefully at Shane. "Do you think I could have a cookie now?"

"Sure."

Dante watched them walk off. "You have a weird family."

"Tell me about it."

"You'd be a cute elf. Do you think the costume has pointy ears?" He sounded hopeful as he asked the question.

"You have a thing for pointy ears?"

"No, but I'm picturing an elf costume. It's very sexy."

"You're as strange as my family."

"I can live with that."

He leaned in as if he was going to kiss her, but just then a voice came over the speaker system.

"Hello, everyone. I'm Mayor Marsha. Welcome to the annual Fool's Gold tree lighting ceremony."

Dante straightened. "Later," he promised.

She nodded.

The crowd moved in around them. Dante shifted her so she was in front of him, his arms around her waist. She leaned into him, enjoying the contact and the warmth.

After a few minutes of announcements, a song from the high school glee club, a cheer from the

high school cheerleaders and a drum roll, the lights
of the thirty-foot tree came on.

They shone brightly against the dark night sky,
and the crowd clapped. There was a bright star at
the top, and about half the lights blinked on and
off. A few feet away, a little boy asked, "Daddy,
do you think it's gonna snow?"

Everyone laughed.

Unfortunately, the skies were clear. Evie found
herself agreeing with the little boy—wanting snow
on a magical night.

"I have so got to get me one of those," Dante
whispered in her ear.

She laughed. "Where would you put it?"

"I'm not sure, but I'd figure something out."

AN HOUR LATER they were back at her place. With
the gas fireplace going and the heat up, they'd
finally stopped shivering. Without jackets and
scarves getting in the way, they could do some
very interesting things with each other, as Evie
discovered, stretched out on the sofa with Dante.

He had his arms around her and his body pressed
to hers. He was all lean muscle—masculine and
strong. When he kissed her, she found herself more
than willing to surrender. The idea of being sensible was highly overrated.

He kissed her cheek, her jaw and then down
her neck. Shivers accompanied the brush of his

mouth. Very specific parts of her body were paying attention, and she found herself willing him
to touch her breasts.

She wrapped her arms around him and squirmed
to get closer, hoping he would get the message. He
shifted so he was kissing her mouth again, his
tongue tangling with hers. Passion coiled around
them, drawing them together.

One of his legs slipped between hers. His thigh
pressed against her center. She pushed against the
unyielding surface, wanting the contact, the sweet-
ness of his fingers or even his mouth. The image
of them naked together filled her mind and made
her catch her breath.

He was hard already. She could feel that part
of him pressing against her hip. They were both
adults. Single. There was no reason not to—

He sat up and stared at her. "I should, ah, go."

It sounded like more of a question than a statement. She could see the battle raging in his eyes.
No doubt the fact that his business partner was her
brother had something to do with it. And that he'd
met her mother. He was being sensible. She should
respect that. Which she did. Sort of.

"Okay," she murmured.

"Unless you want me to stay."

She raised her eyebrows. "Did you want me to
order takeout? Are you hungry?"

One corner of his mouth turned up. "Now you're messing with me again."

"Uh-huh."

"I expected better."

"No, you didn't."

He grinned. "Was that a yes on me staying?"

She reached for the hem of her sweater and pulled it slowly over her head. As she moved, she felt him stiffen. What she knew and he didn't was that underneath she wore a camisole. She was still completely covered.

Still, as he stared at her, he looked like a man who had just discovered a miracle.

"That was a yes," she whispered as he reached for her.

Ten

EVIE CARRIED A pot of coffee and a plate of toast upstairs. She was tired in the best possible way. Lack of sleep due to a charming, handsome man in her bed was an excuse she could fully embrace. She walked into the bedroom and set the plates and coffee on the dresser. She pulled two mugs out of her robe pockets. Before she could pour, Dante stepped out of the bathroom…naked.

He smiled when he saw her. "You're back."

"Are you surprised? I said I would return with coffee."

"I would have been just as happy to see you if you'd come back without any."

He crossed the space between them, took the mugs from her and put them on the dresser, then pulled her into his arms. As she stepped into his embrace, he pushed off her robe and she let it fall to the floor.

Then his hands were touching her, and she

was leaning in to have a little personal contact of her own.

They'd made love twice in the night, then slept in a tangle of arms and legs. She would have thought he was the type to disappear after the deed, but he'd settled in and she'd been happy to have him stay. Now as he slid his hands over her hips and then up to her breasts, she felt herself starting to melt again. But just as they started to kiss, her stomach growled.

Dante drew back. "You didn't get any dinner last night, did you?"

Food hadn't seemed very important. "I'm fine."

"No way. You're not starving on my watch."

He picked up the robe and draped it around her shoulders, then pushed her toward the bed. She pulled her long hair out of the way, shrugged into the robe and slipped between the sheets. After pouring them each a mug of coffee, he carried one to her and handed her the plate of toast.

"Eat."

"Yes, sir."

He returned with his own mug and settled next to her on the bed. He sipped coffee and watched her finish a piece of toast.

"Better?" he asked when she'd finished.

She nodded. "Like I said, I'm fine."

"You're thin and you spend your day dancing. You need more food."

"I weigh nearly ten pounds more than I did when I was dancing professionally."

He leaned back in mock surprise. "And yet the earth manages to stay in its rotational orbit. Stunning."

She grinned. "You think you're funny."

"I am funny." He touched her face. "You're so beautiful."

"That's the sex talking."

"No, it's me." He leaned toward her. "Maybe later you can model some of your ballet costumes."

She laughed.

"See," he told her triumphantly. "I'm funny."

"You're a riot."

"I'm not kidding about the costumes."

She pushed him onto the pillows, then bent over and kissed him. "Do you have a dancer fantasy?"

"No, I have a fantasy about you. It's specific. It's also my favorite."

She knew he was playing, but his words were oddly touching. "I've never been anyone's fantasy before."

"Sure you have," he said before he kissed her. "You just didn't know." His mouth lingered. Then he drew back and pointed to the toast. "Eat more. You'll need to keep your strength up for later."

"That sounds interesting."

He watched her nibble on the toast, then grabbed

a piece for himself. "So why isn't there a guy?" he asked between bites. "A husband or a boyfriend?"

"I haven't met anyone I can imagine falling in love with. Not in a forever kind of way." She shrugged. "I've gotten close a couple of times, but somehow my heart never quite flung itself over the cliff."

"Interesting visual."

She grinned. "You know what I mean."

"I do."

She finished her toast and tied her robe more tightly around her midsection. "What's your story? Why isn't there a Mrs. Jefferson waiting in a suburban paradise somewhere?"

"I'm not that guy," he said with a shrug.

"Don't believe in love?"

"Love is too dangerous." Dante put down his mug of coffee on the nightstand and looked at her. "I was in a gang when I was a kid. I got in early. It was a way to be safe on the streets. My mom didn't like it, but she was working all the time, so she couldn't stop me. Plus I was a kid and pissing her off didn't matter."

He took her hand in his and stared at their linked fingers. "When I was fifteen, I met a girl. She belonged to a rival gang leader, but we didn't care. We were in love. And stupid. When he found out, he went after my mom."

Dante raised his head and looked into her eyes.

"She was killed in a drive-by shooting. To teach me a lesson."

If Evie had been standing, she would have fallen. She could feel her legs giving way and her breathing stop.

"I stole a car to go after him," he continued. "I was caught and instead of being put into jail, I went into a trial program that pulled younger teens out of the gang world and put them in a completely different environment. For me, that was a military school in Texas."

"I'm sorry," she whispered and reached for him. She put her hands on his shoulders and lightly kissed him. "I'm so sorry."

"Thanks. I don't talk about her much. It was a long time ago, but I still miss her."

"Of course you do."

She couldn't comprehend what he'd told her. The words all made sense, but the images were painful, and she was picturing them from a distance.

"I would give anything to have her back," he said quietly. "She was so good to me, and I was a typical teenager. She never got to see me grow up."

"She would have been really proud of you."

"I know." He glanced at her. "I'm not prepared to put my heart in someone else's hands again, but she's the main reason I've pushed you about

May. I would give anything for a second chance with my mom."

The situations were different, but she understood how he would think that. "I can see how you'd want to ride to the rescue. You do that a lot."

"Me? Never."

"You, always."

He kissed her. "Don't make me too much of the good guy." He paused. "I meant what I said before. I don't talk about this. Rafe doesn't know." He hesitated.

She squeezed his hand. "I won't say anything to anyone."

"Thanks."

He drew her down next to him and kissed the side of her neck. "Enough with the serious topics. What are your plans for today?"

She snuggled close, thinking she would happily give up all her plans to spend more time with him. But she wasn't going to push or assume.

"I have laundry," she said. "I might go buy a Christmas tree later, and I have nothing to eat in the house but a loaf of bread and coffee."

"Sounds like a full day," he said, leaning over her. His blue eyes sparkled with something she would like to think was passion and maybe a little anticipation. "Any room for me in it?"

"What did you have in mind?" she asked, her voice breathless.

"A lot of things." He brushed his mouth against hers.

She wrapped her arms around his neck and gave herself over to the sensations washing through her. His hand fumbled with the tie on her robe, then the silky fabric fell free. His fingers caressed her belly before moving higher and—

She stiffened, sure she'd heard something from downstairs.

"What was that?" she asked.

Dante raised his head. "It sounded like voices."

"And footsteps."

She wasn't the type to hear bumps in the night. Besides, it was practically midmorning on a weekend. The sun was out and people were around.

"I'll go investigate," Dante said, sitting up. He reached for his jeans, but before he could pull them on, the bedroom door was pushed open and her brothers rushed inside.

"Are you all—"

Rafe had been speaking. Now his mouth fell open as he stared. Three pairs of eyes widened in identical expressions of astonishment. Evie had a feeling she looked just as shocked.

"You're naked," Clay said at last, obviously horrified by the realization.

All Evie had needed to do was hold her robe closed, but Dante had no such luck. He was caught, sitting on the edge of her bed, jeans in one hand, and that was it.

Rafe's gaze narrowed. "You're sleeping with my sister? We talked about that."

Evie scrambled to her feet and stepped in front of Dante. "You so did not. Because there is no way you have the right to get involved in my personal life. And just because you're paying for this town-house doesn't mean you have the right to enter un-announced."

Rafe ignored her. "I told you to check on her. To look after her."

Evie spun to face Dante, who was pulling on his jeans. "He told you that?"

Dante stood and fastened his pants. "He men-tioned something about it." His gaze settled on her. "You know that's not why I'm here."

She paused, then nodded briefly. "I do. It's okay."

"It's not okay," Shane told her. "Nothing about this is okay."

She turned toward her brothers. "No. You don't get to dictate my personal life. You gave up that right a long time ago and you know it."

She expected them to back off. It wasn't as if

they could have much of an argument. But Clay actually stepped forward.

"Evie, don't you get it? You're our sister and we love you."

FIVE MINUTES LATER Dante finished dressing. Evie had sent her brothers to the kitchen to wait. She drew a sweater over her head, then pulled her hair free. Dante pulled her into his arms.

"Freaked out?" he asked.

"A little."

"Sorry that had to happen. Families are a complication."

She nodded, knowing in this case, he didn't have a problem with complications. She knew he would do anything to have his mom back. Because of that, she wasn't about to complain about her brothers showing up the way they did.

"I'll see you later?" he asked.

"I'd like that."

"Why don't I come over around five with take-out and a movie," he told her. "We can have a quiet evening in."

She stepped into his embrace and hung on for a second. Dante was strong and warm and the kind of guy she would find it easy to fall for. Not that it would be a smart move. After all, he'd made it clear he didn't do long-term, and she had spent years loving people who wouldn't love her back.

He kissed her and then stepped back. "Come on. You can walk me to the door so no one feels compelled to attack."

"Probably for the best," she said, taking his hand in hers. "Clay knows martial arts. I think he could kill you with a matchbook cover."

Dante winced. "I really didn't need to know that."

She laughed.

Her good humor lasted until they reached the living room. Dante grabbed his jacket and left, while she had to go face her brothers.

She hesitated, confused by Clay's seemingly earnest words.

They loved her? That was news, as far as she was concerned. They didn't act as if they loved her. Until she'd been forcibly moved to Fool's Gold after her injury, she hadn't seen any of them in over a year. Except for Rafe, who had shown up in the early part of the summer.

She wanted to say it didn't matter, except she kind of liked the idea of having family who cared. She'd been alone for what felt like forever.

No, she told herself firmly. She wasn't getting sucked in to home and hearth and all that crap. It was the season and Fool's Gold. The town was holiday obsessed. How was she supposed to maintain a sensible amount of emotional reserve when she was going to things like tree lighting ceremonies?

She drew in a breath, then walked purposefully into the kitchen. Her brothers sat at the bar stools by the counter. They each had a mug of coffee and plates littered with dark crumbs. Her lone bag of bread was now crumbled and empty.

"You don't have a lot of food around here," Shane said. "You need to go to the store. Toast isn't breakfast."

Clay nodded at the refrigerator. "You don't even have milk."

"I drink my coffee black."

"Why?"

She sighed. "You can't do this. You can't show up with no warning."

"Because we might find you in bed with a guy?" Rafe asked flatly. "I don't like you sleeping with Dante."

Evie faced him. "You don't get a vote. I'm over eighteen."

"That's not the point."

"It's exactly the point. He's a good guy. I like him. It's not your business."

"I work with him."

"Then don't ask how his weekend was because, believe me, you don't want details."

Clay stood and leaned toward her. "Is it a money thing?"

Evie stared at him, unable to grasp what he was asking. Then she realized he was still talking about the lack of food in her refrigerator and not her reasons for sleeping with Dante.

"It's not money. I don't keep food in the house because if it's here, I'll eat it."

Shane picked up his mug. "What else would you do with food?"

Clay punched him in the arm. "It's about weight, moron." He turned back to her. "You need to eat. You're too thin."

"Is that possible?" she asked, trying to go for humor and suspecting she failed.

"You're not dancing anymore, Evie," Clay told her. "It's okay to be like everyone else."

"Is that what you're doing?"

He patted his stomach. "Charlie's making sure of it."

She waved her hand. "Okay, whatever." She looked at all of them. "While I appreciate the effort, you can't barge in here without calling first. Understood?"

They nodded.

"We wanted to surprise you," Rafe said.

"Then you achieved your goal."

He studied her. "Evie, I know it was bad before. When we were kids."

It had been, she thought. She could be mad at them forever, but to what end? They were her brothers. They'd had their own growing up to do. She'd been a lot younger and the only girl.

"We all did the best we could," she told him.

For a second she thought one of them might ask the inevitable "Even Mom?" But none of them did. Shane walked around the counter and pulled her close. Clay and Rafe joined in for the group hug. For the first time in as long as she could remember, her brothers held her.

When they'd released her, she smiled at Rafe. "Just so you know, I wasn't a virgin."

He groaned and covered his ears with his hands. "Stop! You have to stop."

Clay chuckled. "Feeling pretty good about yourself, aren't you?"

"I am."

Eleven

LATE MONDAY MORNING, Evie parked in front of the Fool's Gold animal shelter. There was a large sign stating that over nine hundred and forty-seven animals had been adopted by the community and that donations were always welcome. When she got out of the car, she heard a couple dozen dogs barking and figured the meeting would be loud, if nothing else.

She walked toward the front door. Another car drove in and she recognized her mother's Mercedes. As May got out of her car, Evie braced herself for whatever was to come. She was relatively sure her brothers would have shared the details of their visit to her place the previous morning. She wasn't exactly thrilled about discussing her sex life with her mother, but she wasn't sure she could actually get out of the conversation.

She waited for her mother to join her. May smiled broadly as she approached.

"This is going to be so exciting," she said happily. "I can't wait to meet all the animals. Rina was telling me that last year there was an iguana up for adoption. Though she said she decided not to give it any special beauty treatment for the holidays."

"Aren't iguanas huge?" Evie asked. "What was she going to do? Paint its toenails?"

"As long as she doesn't expect us to do that."

They walked inside and were met by a pretty young woman in her mid-twenties.

"Hi. I'm Tammy Blalock. I work here at the shelter." Tammy smiled. "I also have a shift at Starbucks. So if you think you've seen me around town, you have."

"You keep busy," May said.

"I know. Life's more fun that way."

"Nice to meet you," Evie said, suddenly feeling like a slacker.

"Rina's already here," Tammy said, leading them through the small office and into the back of the building. "She's putting together a list of who we have to put up for adoption. We already have pictures up on our website and we've done some holiday graphics."

Tammy's long blond ponytail swung as she walked. Evie and May followed her into an open area with a thick outdoor rug and several low chairs. There were also toys and a feline climbing post.

"This is our biggest greeting area," Tammy told them. "Where potential pet parents can spend time with some of our residents. Cats are this way and dogs are over there."

As she spoke, she pointed at two different doors. One had a big cat painted on it, the other had a grinning cartoon beagle.

"Rina's in with the cats," Tammy continued and held open the appropriate door.

Evie and May walked inside. There were dozens of large, airy cages and nearly as many cats. Calicos and marmalades, tabbies and cats in solid colors. Some were sleeping, a few kittens were playing together in one of the larger cages. Evie was immediately drawn to a black-and-white long-haired tuxedo cat with green eyes and a disdainful expression.

Evie crossed to him and offered her fingers for him to sniff. He leaned forward slightly and touched his nose to the edge of her finger, then turned a little, as if offering his cheek. She rubbed his soft fur.

"Hi, handsome," she murmured.

"That's Alexander," Tammy told her. "He's about two or three years old. We're not sure. He was found abandoned and starving a couple of months ago. He's friendly enough around people, but understandably wary. He won't purr for anyone. People want to adopt a cat who purrs."

Alexander looked at her, as if asking if she would be willing to purr, under the circumstances.

"No, I wouldn't," she told him.

Carina McKenzie, otherwise known as Rina, walked into the cat room, clipboard in hand. "Hi, May. Nice to see you again. You must be Evie."

"Hi," Evie said. "Nice to meet you."

"You, too. I really appreciate the help with the adoption. I didn't want to give it up this year, but Dr. Galloway keeps telling me to stay off my feet as much as possible." Rina wrinkled her nose. "She's gotten more stern and is threatening to put me on bed rest if I don't start listening."

Tammy pointed to the door leading back to the getting-to-know-you room just outside the entrance. "Then maybe we should have this conversation out there, where you can sit, young lady."

"Oh, yes. You're right." Rina put her hand on her large belly.

May followed them out. Evie paused, then glanced back at Alexander. The cat stared at her with an expression that said he wasn't the least bit surprised by her leaving. After all, humans hadn't treated him that well. There was no reason for him to trust her, either.

Evie hesitated, then followed the other women out of the cat room.

When they were seated, Rina handed them each several sheets of paper. "This is the layout we used last year at the convention center," she said. "It worked well. The shelter already has the adoptable pets' pictures up on the website. I've got the advertising started. There will be several mentions on the local radio stations and an ad in the local paper. The posters for the storefronts are going to be ready tomorrow."

May had her iPad open. "I already have a note to pick them up and deliver them to the various stores." She smiled. "Glen, Shane and Clay are going to help me. I'm also going to get the flyers."

"Good," Rina said. "We want to hand them out to as many people as possible."

"I would like about a hundred for the dance studio," Evie said. "My students can take them home."

Rina smiled. "Great. Kids are my target audience. Now for the adoption itself. The dogs need to be groomed." She pulled out another list. "Last year I handled most of that, but there's no way I can be on my feet. However, I have a list of volunteers."

Tammy nodded. "I'm heading that group. Rina's been giving me lessons on basic grooming. For ____ think a good br___ ____ brushing is enou___ ____ ___ I'm not touching anything that slithers or crawled." She shuddered.

"Cute matters when it comes to adoptions," Rina told them. "Sad but true. So we want fluffy, great-smelling pets. Now here's what we did last year on the actual day."

They went over how many tables they would need and the layout at the convention center. Rina had another list of volunteers who would be delivering pets that morning. Evie was more than stunned when she realized how many moving parts there were to the event and found herself offering to drive cats and dogs to the venue. She was also surprised at how her mother seemed to have a complete understanding of the logistics involved.

"With luck, everything will be done by one or two in the afternoon," Rina said. "I'll be there, and so will Cameron." She smiled as she mentioned her husband. "He's working very hard to keep me off my feet, so I'm not sure how much help I'll be."

"You need to take care of yourself and your baby," May told her firmly. "We can handle this. Having Tammy to contact will be a big help."

She confirmed a few more details, all the while typing on her iPad.

They wrapped up the last of the details, then May and Evie walked out.

"I enjoyed that," May said. "While I appreciate having plenty of free time these days, I've missed the responsibility of having a job."

"The adoption is a lot more work than I realized," Evie admitted as they stood by their cars. "But I'm glad to be helping. Thanks for asking me."

May smiled at her. "I'm the one who needs to thank you. I couldn't possibly do it all alone. Glen is terrified I'm going to bring home all the animals that don't get adopted, but I've promised I won't. Right now we have travel plans. Getting a new house pet wouldn't be fair to the animal. But Rafe and Heidi are thinking of looking at dogs."

Evie thought about Alexander. She wasn't sure how a cat would fit in her life. She'd never had a pet before and hadn't grown up with them, either. For all her love of animals, May hadn't wanted pets around. Probably because she'd had enough to do with four children and little money, Evie thought. Maybe she should look up cats on the internet and find out what was involved with owning one. The guest room of her townhouse faced south, and there was a small window seat. Didn't cats like to lie in the sun?

They worked out when they would next meet to discuss the event, then Evie started to say goodbye. But before she managed to get out the words, her mother touched her arm.

"I heard about what happened with your brothers and Dante."

Evie had managed to forget the incident while they were helping with the animals, so she was unprepared to have her mother bring it up now. She felt herself flush, which was followed by reminding herself she was an adult and what she did in

her private life was no one's business but her own. As good as the words sounded, however, she didn't exactly remain convinced.

"My brothers need to knock before walking into my house, and I need to make sure the front door is locked," she said.

"Dante seems very nice," her mother said. "I hope you're being smart about things."

Smart? As in not falling for a man who had made it clear he wasn't interested in a relationship? Smart as in...

"You're talking birth control," Evie said slowly, her stomach clenching as an emotional blow hit directly home.

Of course that was something her mother would worry about. She'd had to deal with the consequences of an unplanned pregnancy. The fact that Evie was the result made things a little awkward.

May touched her arm again, this time hanging on. "No," she said quickly. "I'm talking protecting your health. I hear so many scary things on the news about sexually transmitted diseases. Dante has a bit of a reputation and I was worried."

"Oh. You mean condoms. Don't worry. We used them."

May's expression turned sad. "Is that what you think? That I regret having you?"

"Yes."

"Oh, Evie, I don't. I wouldn't change anything."

May sighed. "All right. That's not true. If I could go back in time, I would do so many things differently, when it came to you. I would be there for you and make sure you felt as if you were a part of the family. But I would never, ever not have you. You're my baby girl."

When Clay had mournfully informed her that her brothers loved her, she'd almost been able to believe his words. But with her mother, she was less sure.

"I want to think that's true," she said slowly.

"I know." May squeezed her arm again, then released her. "You're cautious with me, and I understand that. You've been through so much. I just hope you'll give me a chance and the time it's going to take to win you over. I'm not giving up on us, and I'd like you to get to the place where you feel the same way."

Evie nodded slowly, not sure what she felt. May hugged her briefly, then got into her car and drove away.

Evie continued to stand in the parking lot and thought about all the reasons she could still be angry with her mother. Unbidden, a disconcerting thought popped into her head. She was twenty-six. Her mother had only been a few years older when her husband had died, leaving her a widow with three boys and no money. No doubt she'd been terrified and desperately lonely. One night a handsome stranger had come calling, and May had made a mistake.

The man had disappeared the next morning, and a few weeks later, May had discovered she was pregnant.

For the first time ever, Evie tried to understand what that must have been like. No doubt May had been humiliated and ashamed. She would have also been worried about how she was supposed to pay for the birth, not to mention all the things an infant needed.

What her mother had done to her wasn't right, but maybe, just maybe, it was a little understandable. As Dante and Charlie and even her brothers had pointed out, she had to be willing to accept what was offered. To make peace. Being a part of her family wasn't a given—it required work on everyone's part. May had shown she was willing to go more than halfway. Now Evie had to decide how far she was willing to go herself.

DANTE FINISHED GOING OVER the contract. Most people found the idea of a novel-length legal document daunting, but he enjoyed the challenge. Most of the company's business transactions were straightforward. Still, every now and then, someone tried to screw with them. His job was to make sure that person wasn't successful.

He saved the document on his computer, then

printed out a final copy for signature. As the paper spewed out into the tray, Rafe walked around the corner and paused by his desk.

"Have a minute?"

Dante took one look at his friend's face and knew he wasn't going to like whatever Rafe had on his mind. He also had a good idea what the subject was going to be. But Evie was Rafe's sister, so the man deserved to be heard.

"Sure."

Rafe pulled up a chair and sat down.

"Do I need to kill you?" he asked, his voice deceptively calm.

Dante studied his friend. He could challenge the question—Rafe wasn't the murderous type. But Rafe was more than a business partner and he deserved answers.

"Evie and I like each other."

"And that's supposed to make it okay?"

"It's supposed to tell you that I understand why you might be concerned," Dante told him. "Look, we're spending some time together. I didn't mean for it to happen. You're the one who asked me to look out for her."

"Not by sleeping with her. What were you thinking?"

"That she's a beautiful woman with a great sense of humor who shares my ambivalence about the holidays."

Rafe's gaze was steady. "She's my sister and I don't want her hurt."

"We're clear on what we're doing."

"You're clear," Rafe told him. "But I'm worried about her. Evie isn't like you."

Dante looked at his friend. "You sure about that? From what she's told me, no one in her family knows her very well."

Rafe shifted. "That's true, but I know what you're like in a relationship. I don't want that for her."

Dante understood the complaint. Rafe didn't object to Dante's style so much as the inevitable outcome. There was no happy ending. Ever.

"We've discussed ground rules," Dante told him. "But the next time I see her, I'll bring them up again and make sure she and I are on the same page."

"If you're not and she's upset, I'll have to kill you."

Dante slapped him on the back. "There's that holiday spirit."

Rafe glowered at him. "Dammit, Dante. My sister?"

"I'm sorry, Rafe. I tried to remember that she was your sister, but this attraction was mutual."

Rafe grumbled something under his breath and stalked away. Dante sat at his desk, suddenly less sure he'd made himself clear to Evie. He checked his watch. She would be arriving for work in less than an hour. He would talk to her before her classes began and make sure they had the same expectations. He'd meant what he said—he liked her. The last thing he wanted to do was hurt her.

EVIE ARRIVED AT THE dance studio forty-five minutes before her classes started. The first thing she did was crank up the heat. The old building was drafty and cold in winter. If it were up to her, she would relocate the dance studio to a newer place, with a bigger dance floor and maybe a second practice room. As it was, she waited until she heard the telltale whoosh of the furnace starting, then hung her coat on the rack and went over the classes for that day.

They were getting close to the panic period for the production. In less than two weeks, they would start practicing on stage so everyone could perform in the actual location. The stage was considerably wider than their studio, so that would take some getting used to. There was also the seemingly endless rows of chairs. The thought of an audience could be daunting to even a seasoned professional.

She crossed to the stereo system and connected her phone to speakers, then scrolled through her list of music and found a favorite song. She'd just walked over to the barre when Dante walked in.

She smiled as she glanced from the living, breathing, tempting man to his many reflections in the mirror. Both were appealing although she had to admit she preferred the one she could put her hands on.

"Hi," she said, crossing to him.

"Hi, yourself." He rested his hands on her waist and lightly kissed her. "You going to do some fancy dance moves?"

"I haven't warmed up."

"Can I help with that?"

She laughed. "No. I have students arriving in about thirty minutes."

"Bummer." He drew in a breath. "I had a talk with your brother earlier today."

As the two men worked together, that was hardly news. Except he wasn't sharing a part of a day—instead he was passing on information.

She pressed her fingertips against his chest and winced. "I'm sorry. For what it's worth, I had a talk with my mother."

Dante grimaced. "About the pet adoption?"

"Not exactly. She told me to make sure we were using condoms so I wouldn't catch a disease."

"She didn't."

Evie stared into his eyes. "Do I look like I'm lying?"

"Sorry."

"Me, too. About my brother. Not about the other night."

"Me, either." But he didn't sound completely sure.

She carefully lowered her arms to her sides and took a small step back, pulling away from his light touch. "Dante, this isn't the 1800s. One great night doesn't mean we're engaged."

"I know, I just want to make sure we're on the same page."

She could translate easily enough. He wanted to make sure she remembered their time together was meant to be fun. Not a relationship.

She'd been very clear on what they were doing when they'd started hanging out together. So she couldn't complain about being misled. If she'd started to look forward to seeing Dante more than she should, it was her own business, right? If she was hoping for more than a good time, that was her problem.

She continued to watch Dante's face. "You and I are friends. We like each other and are enjoying spending time together. We're both a little freaked out about the town's obsession with being cheerful and embracing every nuance of all things Christmas. Holidays are stressful and we're getting each other through. The other night we discovered that you earned your reputation with women the hard way and I appreciate that. There are no expectations between us. Does that sum it up?"

She spoke lightly, doing her best to sound as blasé and experienced as any other woman he'd been with. The slight jab of pain in the vicinity of her heart didn't have anything to do with him.

"Perfectly." His blue eyes crinkled with amusement. "I'm glad you enjoyed the other night. I did, too."

"See? We're good. Now you ignore my brother and I'll ignore my mother and all will be well."

"Promise," he told her. He gave her a quick kiss. "We'll both be working late tonight. How about lunch tomorrow?"

"I have to help Annabelle with the book drive."

"There's a book drive? Why? Because the town needed one more philanthropic event?"

"I know. But Annabelle called and asked and I couldn't figure out how to say no. Apparently every child in Fool's Gold gets a book for Christmas. They have to be wrapped, so I'm going up to Ronan's Lodge. We're meeting in the Mountain ballroom." She held up both hands. "I didn't have the heart to tell her I'm not very good at wrapping presents."

"We could practice tonight," he suggested. "Wrapping and unwrapping."

A tempting offer, she thought. But one she wasn't sure her heart could risk her accepting. Before she could decide, she heard footsteps on the stairs. Light footsteps from one of her beginning classes. Dante took a step back.

"Later," he mouthed and walked out of the studio.

As Evie greeted her students, she glanced toward the door. Being sensible about Dante was the smartest move. She had to protect herself and her heart. But deep inside, she knew there was a part of her that wanted more. Wanted to believe in someone. To have a little faith and maybe find love.

Twelve

EVIE PARKED IN front of the Fool's Gold Animal Shelter and got out of her car. She'd called ahead to make sure this was a convenient time for the staff, but now she hesitated. Was she really ready to take on the responsibility of caring for a cat?

"I guess that's what I'm here to find out."

Tammy was waiting for her as she walked into the building. Alexander was sitting on a tall, carpeted platform, his long tail swishing as he looked around the room.

"This is the one, isn't it?" Tammy asked. "You said Alexander, but sometimes people get names mixed up."

"This is him."

Evie walked over to the cat and held out her fingers for him to sniff. "Hi, big guy. How are you doing?"

His green eyes narrowed slightly. He took an obligatory sniff, then turned away.

"Does he hate me?" Evie asked, not sure what his actions meant in the cat world. If she were on a blind date, she would know exactly what he was thinking and it wouldn't be flattering.

"He's making you work for it," Tammy told her. "Keep talking to him and then pet him. He's going to make you earn his trust."

"I can respect that," she said, keeping her voice quiet. "If I were you, I wouldn't be very trusting, either."

She lightly touched his back. While he didn't flinch, he wasn't relaxed, either. His shoulders got a little hunchy. She continued to stroke him, moving slowly and gently, not making sudden moves.

The phone rang.

"I need to get that," Tammy told her. "I'll be right back."

Evie nodded and kept her attention on the cat. She lengthened the strokes so she was petting him from shoulder to tail. After a couple of minutes, he relaxed. By the time Tammy returned, he was actually glancing at her with something slightly warmer than disdain.

"I like him," Evie said. "I need to make sure I'm ready for a cat, but I'm leaning in that direction for sure. Has anyone else said they're interested in him?"

"No. He's not a kitten, which makes his adoption more challenging. But I can let you know if we get any calls before the event."

"That would be great." Evie glanced at her watch. "I have to run. Thanks for this, Tammy."

"No problem. I hope you take him. He's a great guy."

"Bye, Alexander."

The cat looked at her. His eyes narrowed slightly as if he realized she was leaving. Then he turned away. Evie wanted to tell him that she might be giving him a forever home, but stopped herself. Until she was sure, it wouldn't be right to allow him to hope. Unfortunately, explaining to herself that Alexander didn't speak English didn't make her feel any less awful about leaving without him.

EVIE WAS ALREADY LATE. She hurried through town on her way to Ronan's Lodge, glancing at her watch as she went. Thoughts of Dante and her family and the production had kept her tossing and turning much of the night. Now she had to face a morning of book wrapping. She hoped there was an instructional session first.

She glanced longingly at the Starbucks as she passed, but there was no time. As she waited to cross at the light, three teenaged girls came out of the coffee place and spotted her.

"OMG! That's her!" A tall blonde in skinny

jeans and a heavy down coat raced toward her. "Ms. Stryker? Could you wait a second?"

The other two girls with her were both brunettes with big eyes and wide smiles. All three of them were clutching to-go drink containers.

The blonde spoke first. "You're Evie Stryker, right?"

Evie nodded slowly.

"This is so cool. I'm Viv and these are my friends Tai and Wendy. We're cheerleaders." Viv's grin broadened. "I'm actually team captain this year."

"Congratulations," Evie said, hoping the uneasy feeling she had in her stomach was uncalled for and that the girls were just being extra Fool's Gold friendly.

Viv held her drink in both hands. "Every year we do a fund-raiser for the squad. We save money to go to cheerleading camp in the summer."

"Okay," Evie said slowly, the unease turning to sinking. "What kind of fund-raiser?"

"We do a Pom-Pom-A-Thon," Tai, or maybe Wendy, said. "People hire us to go to someone's house and do cheers, only they're Christmas related."

The three of them glanced at each other, then shouted together, "Hey, hey, ho, ho. Merry Christmas and away we go."

Viv laughed. "They're not all that lame, I prom-

ise. We were thinking that we're not as good as
we could be. So we've got some friends in the creative writing club helping us with new cheers. We
were wondering if you could help us with some
moves. After all, you were a professional cheerleader, right?"

Evie winced. Her short-lived career as an L.A.
Stallions cheerleader had ended badly and wasn't
anything she wanted to talk about.

"The Stallions' squad was more about dance
than cheering," she said.

The three teens looked at each other, then back
at her. "That's what we want," Viv said. "Some
ideas to add a little fun to our routines. It would
only take a couple of hours. Please."

Evie thought about the book wrapping and the
performance, the students she had to work with
privately, her volunteering for the pet adoption and
how she couldn't seem to take a step without running into someone from her family. This was not
the time to take on one more project.

But as she looked at the girls, she couldn't seem
to summon the word *no*. She sighed. "Sure. I can
help. I have to help wrap books right now and then
maybe after that?"

"You're working with Annabelle?" Viv asked.
"With the book drive? We're going there, too." She
turned to her friends. "We need to work really hard
so Evie can have more time with us."

Which would be great for Annabelle and less thrilling for herself, Evie thought, knowing she might as well simply give in to the inevitable.

The four of them made their way to the hotel. Signs directed them to the ballroom. As Evie stepped through the open double doors, she realized she hadn't known what to expect. A few boxes of books and some tables, maybe. It was that times a thousand.

There were at least forty tables set up. On each one was a box, a roll of gift wrap, tape and a sheet of colored stickers. A small crowd was clustered together near the front of the room. Evie and the cheerleaders joined them.

Heidi was there, along with Patience and Charlie. Jo, from the bar where they'd all had brunch on Thanksgiving. She recognized a few other people from town, along with a few of her students' moms. Annabelle checked her watch, then waved to get everyone's attention.

"Thank you for coming," she said. "I'm hoping this won't take very long. I know the season is busy and I appreciate the time and effort you're offering."

Evie felt a warm hand settle on the small of her back. She turned and saw Dante standing next to her.

"What are you doing here?" she asked in a whisper.

"Rafe was supposed to come, but he's on a conference call that's gone long. I offered to represent the company."

He smiled as he spoke. Evie found herself easing toward him, wanting to press her body against his. Remembering the cheerleaders who were no doubt keeping an eye on her, she forced herself to stand straight and pretend she wasn't tingling from the light touch on her back.

"Every table has a box of books," Annabelle was saying. "They are grouped together by age and gender. So please don't trade books with anyone else. When you've wrapped the book, put one of the stickers on the upper right corner. The sticker tells the age range and whether the book is for a boy or a girl. Again, please don't trade stickers."

"There are a lot of rules," Dante whispered into her ear.

Evie fought off a shiver as her body pointed out that every single part of her really liked what this man could do to her and that it had been a while since they'd seen each other naked.

"Behave," she said.

"I am."

She winced, realizing she'd actually been talking to herself rather than him.

Annabelle sent them off to find tables. The cheerleaders took one together and Dante joined Evie.

"Who are your friends?" he asked, motioning

to the teens who were taking books out of the box and unrolling the paper.

"They're on the high school cheerleading squad. I'm going to help them with a fund-raiser they're doing."

He raised his eyebrows.

"I know, I know." She kept her voice low. "It shouldn't take too much of my time."

"You're in demand," he said. "Impressive."

"Overwhelming."

"How can I help?"

She laughed. "Unless you have a secret background as a cheerleader, I'm not sure you can."

"Hmm, there is that year I spent working undercover. Let me see what I can remember."

She laughed and handed him the first book. "Wrap."

"How about I cut the paper and put on the stickers, and you wrap."

"Chicken."

"These are presents for kids. They should look nice."

"Fine. I'll wrap."

They had picked a table with large picture books. For boys, Evie thought, looking at covers with trucks and bugs and camping raccoons.

"I know most women think about having a little girl," she said, taking the piece of wrapping paper Dante handed her, along with the book he'd cut it for, "but I've always pictured myself with sons. I'm guessing that comes from growing up with three brothers."

"Boys are less complicated," Dante agreed. "They want to do things. Girls have feelings."

She laughed. "Are you saying boys don't?"

"I'm saying I understand what a boy feels. Can you see me sitting at a little table having pretend tea with a four-year-old and her toy bears?"

Evie studied him, taking in the deep blue eyes, handsome face and, as always, well-cut, killer suit. She could totally see Dante falling for a little girl. He would be a protective father, one who kissed a boo-boo to make it better and slayed dragons, be they real or imagined. And, yes, she could imagine him sitting at a too-small table and having pretend tea.

They'd both grown up without a father figure in their lives, so she would guess they both knew how important a dad could be. While children weren't on her immediate radar, should that happen, she would prefer to have a man around. She doubted he was the kind of man who would ever consider walking away from his kids.

Under other circumstances he might be someone she wanted to consider hanging on to. Only Dante wasn't into forever, and she was planning on moving on. Although right now her reasons for wanting to leave Fool's Gold seemed a little fuzzy.

"You'd be great," Evie told him and centered the book on the wrapping paper.

IN LESS TIME THAN Dante would have thought, the books were wrapped. Evie went off with her cheer-leader fans and he stayed after to help load the wrapped books into boxes for delivery.

Gideon joined him, loading the boxes onto a cart.

"Do you know if Evie's gone over my sugges-tions for the production?" he asked.

Dante straightened slowly and stared at the other man. "What are you talking about?"

"I'm doing the narration for *The Dance of the Winter King.* Didn't she tell you?"

"No. She didn't mention it."

Gideon was tall and moved like someone who knew his way around a fight. Dante recognized the subtle signs from his own early years. The scar by Gideon's eyebrow and the tattoo visible under his rolled-up shirtsleeves were also a clue.

"I had some suggestions to make the transitions smoother," Gideon said. "The premise of the story is interesting. I like the message."

"There's a message?"

"Sure. Every child is special. Unique." He gave a quick smile. "Like a snowflake."

A snowflake? Dante did his best to reconcile the dark, dangerous man in front of him with a guy who talked about children being special snow-flakes.

"Okay," he said slowly. "I'll, ah, tell her you're looking for her."

Just then they were joined by a well-dressed, white-haired woman in a suit. It took Dante a moment to put the name with the face.

"Mayor Marsha," he said. "Nice to see you again."

"You, too." The older woman smiled at both of them. "I'm happy to see you're settling in. And you've met Gideon." She turned to the other man. "I'm delighted by the Christmas music. Very eclectic choices. Some traditional songs, of course, but I'm very much enjoying the international selections."

"I like to mix it up," Gideon told her, winking as he spoke. "Keep folks guessing."

The mayor glanced at Dante. "Gideon has recently purchased the two radio stations in town. One AM, one FM. The FM station is playing all Christmas music."

"I'll have to tune in," Dante said politely.

"I'm getting lots of good feedback," Gideon said. "A few local rockers have been by, requesting something else."

"There are local rockers in Fool's Gold?" Dante tried to imagine them being happy in the quiet, family friendly town and couldn't.

"Young rockers," Gideon said, then nodded at the cart. "I need to get these out to the truck. Good to see you, Mayor Marsha."

"You, too."

Dante expected the old lady to move on, but she waited until Gideon had left, then turned to him.

"You're settling in well."

He stared at her, not sure if she was asking a question or making a statement.

"This town is very special," she continued. "A lot is expected of our citizens, but then people get so much in return. Do you know very much about Gideon?"

"No. We've only met a couple of times."

"A very interesting man with a violent history. Then he met a couple of men who changed his life forever. Ford and an angel." She smiled. "Sorry. I couldn't resist."

"I don't get the joke."

"Ford and Angel are men's names. Two men who—" She shook her head. "It's not important. Suffice it to say Ford is the son of one of our founding families. He's coming back, as soon as he figures out how to embrace his past. As for Angel, he'll be home soon, too."

She motioned to the rapidly emptying room. "This is exactly what you need, Mr. Jefferson. You've been on your own for too long. I understand why you've been reluctant to truly settle and admit you're ready to make a home. But here in Fool's Gold we take care of our own. You will always be safe, always welcome."

He stared at the old woman, telling himself there was no way she could know about his past. That no one but Evie knew about his mother and he was convinced she wouldn't have said a word. The mayor was talking in generalities. He was reading too much into her words. Or maybe she was really fishing for information.

He ignored the compassion and certainty in her blue eyes and gave her a practiced smile. "I like Fool's Gold well enough, but I still have my place in San Francisco."

"You'll sell it soon. You belong here, Mr. Jefferson. Fool's Gold has everything you've been looking for. We can't undo the past, but we can heal from it. Oh, and would you please tell May that Priscilla would be more than welcome at the Live Nativity."

The change of subject had him scrambling to catch up. "Excuse me?"

"The Live Nativity. May will worry about Priscilla being left home alone on Christmas Eve Day. She's welcome. Along with her pony."

"You do realize Priscilla is an elephant?"

"Of course."

"In a nativity?"

"God loves all His creatures."

"Won't that look strange?"

"It will look welcoming. No one should be alone for Christmas, Mr. Jefferson. Not even an elephant."

"How is May supposed to get her here?"

"She can walk. It's not that far. Just make sure Heidi doesn't offer to ride her. I don't think that would be a good idea."

He honestly didn't know what to say. He'd seen the stage where the Live Nativity would be on Christmas Eve Day. There was room for Priscilla on either side, along with her pet pony. But still.

Dante drew in a breath. He might never have lost in court, but he recognized a moment when he should simply accept defeat.

"I'll pass along the message."

"Thank you." She touched his arm. "I'm so glad you're here, and we're very lucky to have you as a part of our Fool's Gold family."

She smiled, released him and left. Dante was left standing in the center of the empty room, feeling as if he'd been run over by a freight train. What had just happened? And why did he suddenly want to hug everyone?

Grumbling to himself that the old lady was crazy, he stalked out of the ballroom and headed back to the office. He needed some quality time with a legal brief. That would set his world to rights. Then he could forget all this Christmas crap and get back to being himself.

Thirteen

EVIE WROTE DOWN another idea for a cheer, then pushed away the paper. She had to focus on her production, and time was ticking. There were less than three weeks until *The Dance of the Winter King,* and she was starting to panic. While helping the cheerleaders was fun, she had to remember her responsibility to her students and the town. Of course, when she thought of it in those terms, she got a little sick to her stomach.

A distraction appeared in the form of footsteps on the stairs. It was several hours until her first lesson, but she'd received an email from Dominique Guérin, her boss. Dominique was flying in for the holidays and had said she would like to stop by the studio that morning.

Another thing to be nervous about, Evie thought, automatically standing, her back straight, her feet in first position. Miss Monica, who had sold the dance studio to Dominique over the summer, had been running the school for years. Evie had only been teaching for a couple of months and had never run anything. For all she knew, Dominique was going to fire her.

"Cheerful, upbeat attitude," she murmured, telling herself not to go looking for trouble. After all, it seemed to have no problem finding her. Besides, she'd met Dominique before, and the woman had been very friendly. Of course, back then, Evie hadn't been in charge.

The door opened and Dominique swept inside. Evie resisted the urge to curtsy in the presence of greatness, instead offering a smile and a handshake.

"Dominique," she said. "It's lovely to see you."

Dominique Guérin had to be close to sixty, but she looked as if she were in her forties. Petite, beautiful, with short gold-blond hair and large eyes, she moved with a dancer's sureness and elegance. She'd been more than a great artist, she'd been a star. She'd graced every famous stage in every country, had danced for presidents and kings and been awarded nearly every honor possible. There were rumors of a title, bestowed by Queen Elizabeth, but Evie couldn't get confirmation on that.

"Evie!" Dominique moved close and hugged her. "You look wonderful. So young. I'm jealous. How are you doing? I read all your emails about

Monica. Running off with a man, at her age. I don't know if I should be impressed or worried about her hip."

Dominique smiled. "But if he's her great love, she shouldn't ever look back. Everyone deserves a great love. Of course, she's left us in a bit of a pickle."

"That's one way to describe it," Evie murmured, offering Dominique a chair.

She'd already made tea and now poured them each a mug, then settled across from her boss and sent out a quick request to the universe that the meeting go well.

Dominique shrugged out of her faux-fur coat and draped it over the back of her chair. Evie eyed the other woman's fitted turtleneck and slim jeans. She doubted Dominique had put on a pound since her dancing days.

Dominique picked up her mug of tea. "Fool's Gold is so pretty. I've been in New York, and while it's beautiful there during the holidays, I do love the small town feel here. And there's plenty going on."

Evie gave a strangled laugh. "Sure. The pet adoption, the book drive, hayrides out at the ranch, the day of giving and, hey, *The Dance of the Winter King.* It's busy."

Dominique smiled at her. "You sound overwhelmed."

"Just some days. I'm supposed to help out with the hayrides. I've been told I'm elf material. And I'm also working on the pet adoption. That's on the fifteenth. It's a lot to get through."

"It is. I wonder if Charlie and Clay would like a pet." Dominique leaned toward her. "Clay and I have been talking. He wants a big wedding. Something the town can be involved in. Charlie wants to elope. She says she's not bride material."

"She would be a beautiful bride," Evie said, thinking her future sister-in-law wasn't traditionally feminine but was still her favorite of the three. Although Heidi and Annabelle had certainly been nice enough.

"We'll see who wins the argument," Dominique said. "I'm betting Clay surprises us all, and Charlie gives in. Either way, a dog might be nice for them. Practice before they give me a grandchild."

Dominique sighed. "I can't believe I'm happy about that, but I am. Charlie has told me to stop asking if she's pregnant. She says they're going to wait at least a year. I've tried to remind her that my wants are more important than hers, but she's not listening. It's very wonderful to have family. You must be pleased to be so close to yours."

"You have no idea," Evie murmured, hoping Dominique didn't press for details. "Are you staying in town through the holidays?"

"Yes. I'm very much looking forward to the production."

Evie pressed her hand against the sudden knot in her stomach. "Great. I've made a few changes from what's been done in the past."

She detailed her thoughts on the transitions and how she wanted to make the story tighter. "The voice-over is being modified, as well. A local businessman is helping with that. He owns the radio stations in town."

"Excellent. I adore community involvement. Charlie mentioned the sets had been refurbished."

"They were. We had a work day." Evie told her about that.

"You do have a challenge on your hands," her boss told her. "I would imagine not every student is gifted."

"Some have to work harder than others," Evie admitted. "I'm working with a few girls privately so they can be in the show. It's not that they aren't willing to work hard," she said, not sure how to delicately share the truth.

"But they have no ability or rhythm," Dominique said drily. "I can imagine. Dance is a gift and given to so few. Normally I would be against lowering the standards. After all, this studio has my name on it. But in this case, the production is for the town. Accommodations must be made—in the spirit of the season."

"Exactly," Evie said.

"You're doing an excellent job. I'm very pleased. You stepped in and took control when you could have simply thrown up your hands and said it wasn't your responsibility."

"I didn't want the students to be disappointed." Evie drew in a breath. "I'm very much enjoying teaching."

"Then you're right where you need to be, aren't you?" Dominique glanced around. "This is a grim little studio, isn't it? Old and drafty. After the holidays, I want you and I to talk, Evie. I'm considering buying a building and putting the studio in it. We would have it redone to our exact specifications. Expand, even. Hire a few more teachers. I'd like you to be thinking about any suggestions you have and if you'd like to be in charge."

Evie stared at her. "But I've only been working for you a couple of months."

"I know, but I like what I see. Believe me, I'm used to sizing people up quickly. I had to know if I could trust my partner not to step all over me, figuratively or literally. I would like us to work together. As partners." Dominique sipped her tea, then nodded. "Interesting. Yes, I think we could be partners. After all, we're practically family, and we will be when Charlie marries Clay."

Evie honestly didn't know what to say. The offer thrilled her. She had dozens of ideas for a new studio and just as many suggestions for different classes.

"Thank you," she stammered. "That's so nice of you."

"Nice?" Dominique raised her eyebrows. "How delicious. I've become a nice person. It's strange, but oddly satisfying."

She rose. "I must go and find Charlie. I wouldn't tell her when I was arriving, so it would be a surprise. She'll be both pleased to see me and slightly annoyed that I kept her guessing." Dominique laughed. "A perfect combination."

She reached for her coat, then paused. "Oh, Evie, please get this sad little studio some Christmas decorations. Use the company credit card. Go wild. I want my girls to be excited when they walk in here."

Dominique smiled again, tossed her coat over her shoulder and swept out of the room. Evie was left in the chair, slightly breathless, as if she'd just survived a small tornado.

Her mind hopped from topic to topic, unable to settle. There was too much to consider.

The Christmas decorations were easy enough. She would ask Dante to help her get a tree. Buying ornaments would be fun. As for the rest of what Dominique had said, Evie wasn't sure. The new studio would be wonderful. As for being a partner, the offer was tempting. Despite her slightly odd ways, Dominique was brilliant and easy to work for. But accepting meant staying, and Evie had always planned to leave Fool's Gold.

Staying would mean being around her family, which was both good and bad. Staying meant being a part of the town, of craziness every Christmas. Staying meant complications with Dante. She'd gone into their relationship with the idea she was leaving. If she didn't, how would things end?

Staying meant belonging.

Evie stood and carried both mugs into the small bathroom. She washed them in the sink and dried them before putting them back into the cupboard. Staying meant reconciling with her mother and accepting that, while May had made mistakes, she was genuinely sorry and wanted to make amends. It meant letting go of the anger she'd carried with her like a talisman.

Perhaps the healthiest decision, Evie realized. But without the hurt and anger, she wasn't sure who she would be.

"I GUESS I DIDN'T think this part through," Evie admitted, trying not to laugh.

Dante obviously didn't find anything about the situation amusing. Probably because he was tired and hungry and wasn't the kind of guy to enjoy shopping for a Christmas tree.

Or maybe it wasn't the shopping itself, but the

fact that she'd asked him to carry a seven-foot-tall tree three blocks in the cold and then drag it up a flight of stairs to the studio.

Narrow stairs, where the too-large tree was now stuck.

"I'm sorry," Evie said, staring up through the branches at the scowling man. "Seriously."

"Uh-huh. You're not sorry. You're having fun."

She bit the inside of her lip in an attempt to keep from smiling. "No, I'm not."

"Right." He grabbed the thick trunk with both hands. "I'm going to give this thing one more try. If I can't get it to move, I'll resign myself to slowly starving to death up here."

He kind of had a point, she thought, realizing the tree blocked the only way up or down.

"On three," she said, taking hold of the top of the tree and planning to push.

"Don't help," Dante told her.

"I'm helping."

"You'll get hurt. I can do this."

As he spoke, he began to pull. Despite his instructions, she pushed from the top. Nothing happened. She pushed harder and felt a little bit of give.

"One more time," she yelled.

"Stop help—"

But it was too late. She shoved, he pulled and the tree suddenly moved free, zipping up the stairs, hitting Dante in the center of his chest. They both went sprawling.

Evie found herself flying forward. She braced herself on her hands and landed somewhat gently on the stairs, facedown.

"You okay?" she asked, almost afraid to stand up and look.

"Fine." Dante's voice was slightly strangled.

"I'm going to order a pizza. Pepperoni all right with you?"

"Sure."

She rolled onto her back and pulled her cell phone out of her pocket, then called the local pizza place and put in their order. After she'd hung up, she stood and brushed off the needles decorating the front of her coat. Finally, she risked looking upstairs.

Dante still lay on his back, the tree on top of him, the base of its trunk maybe three inches from his chin.

"Want to talk about it?" she asked.

"Not really."

She went upstairs and helped roll the tree off of him. He rose and glanced down at the tree on the floor and the layer of needles everywhere.

"Whose idea was this?" he asked.

"My boss's."

"I admire her willingness to delegate."

An hour later the tree was in the stand and the

lights were strung. When the pizza guy arrived, Dante disappeared downstairs to pay him and returned with a pizza box, a bottle of wine and two wineglasses.

"I didn't order wine," she said. "Do they deliver wine?"

"They do not. We have a small wine cellar in the office."

"Because you never know when you're going to need a bottle of merlot to get through the day?"

"Something like that."

While she served their pizza, he opened the wine and then poured. They settled across from each other and each grabbed a slice. The scent of pine mingled with the fragrance of cheese and pepperoni.

"Wine, pizza and a Christmas tree," she said. "What's not to like?"

"Can I get back to you on that?"

"Don't be a Grinch. You know this is fun."

His blue eyes brightened with amusement. "You're fun. Is that enough?"

"It works for me."

He glanced at the tree, then back at her. "You've been talking about getting one of those for your place. Still thinking it's a good idea?"

"I am. I'm also thinking of getting a cat."

"As a decoration?"

"I'm not sure he would like that idea."

"He? You've got a cat in mind?"

She thought about the black-and-white one she'd seen at the shelter. Despite how busy she'd been, he kept popping into her mind.

"Sort of. He was very sweet and needs a forever home." She was still getting used to the idea.

"Cats are okay," Dante said, surprising her.

"I would have thought you were the dog type. You know, slavish devotion and someone to play fetch with."

"I don't have any burning desire to play fetch, and I respect how cats make you earn their interest. Cats are like lawyers. Discreet, quiet and watchful."

She managed to keep from choking as she laughed. "You're a weird guy. You know that, right?"

"It's been hinted at before." He looked at the tree. "Your students are going to be excited."

"I'm sure it will help with the holiday spirit." She thought about what he'd told her about his upbringing. "What were Christmases like when you were a kid?"

He shrugged and reached for his glass of wine. "Quiet. Good. We didn't have a lot of money and it was just my mom and me, but we had fun. We went to midnight services on Christmas Eve. I understood we were poor and didn't expect a lot, but

Mom always made the day special." He hesitated. "I miss her at the holidays."

Evie nodded. "Sure. She was your family."

"She would have liked you."

Evie told herself not to read too much into the statement. "Thank you. I would have loved to have met her."

He sipped his wine. "What about you and your family?"

"Christmases were loud," she said, remembering her brothers getting the family up early to see all the presents. There were other memories—times when she'd felt left out, but she wasn't in the mood to explore them.

"After my mom died and I was sent to the military school, Christmas was different," Dante said. "They kept us on campus. My senior year, one of the sponsors invited a couple of us to his house for Christmas." He reached for another slice of pizza and grinned. "Let's just say it's the first time I figured out the rich really are different."

"Nice house?"

"Nice mansion. It was three stories, I don't know how many bedrooms. I'd never seen a tree that big, even at the mall. The family had presents for us and a stocking. I'd never had a stocking before."

"We always had stockings," Evie said, remembering her twelfth Christmas, when her mother

had given her lip gloss and mascara. An acknowl-
edgement that the teen years weren't that far away.

There were good memories, she reminded herself. Maybe instead of focusing on the ones that
were bad, she should start looking for the more
pleasant ones.

"Have you talked to Gideon?" Dante asked, his
voice casual.

"About the narration? Not yet. He left me a message. I need to call him back. He said he has some
ideas about the story. Why?"

"He mentioned it at the book wrapping."

She glanced at Dante, wondering if she was
imagining things or if he genuinely wasn't pleased
about her working with Gideon. In your dreams,
she thought, taking a sip of her wine. While the
idea of Dante jealous was kind of exciting, reality was very different. He'd made it clear what he
was and wasn't looking for in their relationship.
Them being together was all about getting through
the holidays, about having fun together. Neither of
them was committed to anything else, and if she
allowed herself to think anything different, she
was opening herself up to a world of hurt.

Fourteen

"EXTEND," EVIE SAID, holding out her arm to demonstrate. "Reach and lift." She turned slowly, then sank down into the final move.

Lillie smiled. "You're so good," she said with an easy smile. "When you do it, it looks right."

"It looks right when you do it, too." Evie stepped behind the girl so they were both facing the mirror. "Now lift and reach and lift."

She moved with Lillie, lightly pressing her palm against the girl's back to keep her straight.

"Lean, turn, stretch."

Lillie did as instructed. She made one last turn and sank down, her fingertips curled delicately, her wrists perfectly bent.

"See," Evie said approvingly. "That was perfect."

Lillie jumped to her feet and spun in a circle. "I got it! I got it!"

"Look at you," Patience said, walking in to the studio.

"Mom!" Lillie ran to her mother, her arms outstretched. "Did you see me?"

"I did. Lillie, that was beautiful."

Lille dashed off to collect her coat. Patience turned to Evie.

"Thanks for working with her. I know she doesn't get the steps as quickly as the other girls."

"She works hard and has fun. As long as she's enjoying the classes, I'm thrilled to have her. She's a great kid."

"Thank you."

Evie knew that Dominique would say Lillie was one of the "unfortunates." Those not blessed with the dancing gene. But Evie found a special kind of pleasure teaching the Lillies of the world. As far as Evie was concerned, if Lillie enjoyed herself and ended up with good memories about her part in the performance, then the experience was a total success for both of them.

"Are you staying sane?" Patience asked. "I heard the cheerleaders wanted your help with their Pom-Pom-A-Thon."

"I'm running ragged," Evie admitted. "But only a couple more weeks and everything will be done. Then I can collapse through New Year's."

"Tell me about it."

Lillie returned, her boots on her feet and her ballet shoes in her hand. "I'm ready, Mom."

"Okay. Off we go. We have to stop at the grocery store and get more supplies. Your grandmother is still on a cookie tear." Patience waved. "Hang in there and I'll do the same."

"Will do."

She and Lillie left. Evie glanced at the clock. She had about an hour until her next class. Time enough to grab something to eat and maybe stop by Morgan's Books for something to read. As soon as Christmas was over, she was going to put her feet up and not move for a week. There were no classes between the twenty-sixth and the first of the year. While she couldn't afford a real vacation, she could hide out and rest.

"You're starting a cult."

She looked up and saw Dante standing in the doorway to the studio. As always, the sight of him set her heart beating a little faster.

"What are you talking about?" she asked.

"Those girls. You're training them to take over the world."

She laughed. "You're not making any sense."

He walked toward her and took her hand, then led her to the window in the reception area.

"Look down there," he said, pointing. "What do you see?"

"Lillie and Patience."

"And how is Lillie wearing her hair?"

Evie saw the braids tightly wrapped around her head, then reached up and touched her own.

"A coincidence."

"I don't think so. All your students are copying you. It's charming." He put his arm around her and pulled her close. "You're their role model."

"I think I'm more of a cautionary tale."

He kissed the top of her head. "You're being too hard on yourself."

He turned her toward him and kissed her again, this time on her mouth.

"What time's your last class?" he asked.

"I finish at six and then I head over to the ranch for the hayrides."

"Me, too." He groaned. "I'd rather be home, having takeout with you."

"Me, too." She put her hands on his shoulders and stared into his blue eyes. "But instead, you're helping my family. You're a really good guy. I don't usually fall for the good ones. I tend to be attracted to the losers of the world."

He leaned close to whisper in her ear. "It's the sex. You can't help yourself."

Evie was still laughing as he strolled down the stairs.

"I DON'T THINK SO," Evie said, staring at herself in the mirror.

"Come on," Annabelle said, handing over a set of pointed ears. "You look adorable. I can't do it." She patted her belly. "I'm pregnant. How would that look? And Heidi has to handle the petting zoo. You know how the goats get when they have company. They're all so happy, they could accidentally knock over a four-year-old."

Evie stared down at herself. She was wearing a green flared skirt, a long-sleeved red-and-green sweater, along with red-and-white-striped tights. Finishing up the outfit was a green hat and elf ears and pointy green elf shoes.

"I don't want to be an elf," she muttered. "What was I thinking?"

Annabelle beamed at her. "That's the spirit."

"I'm crabby."

"Crabby works, as long as you smile for the pictures. Come on. I just heard a car pull up."

Somehow, when she hadn't been looking, Evie had been roped into helping with the annual hayrides at the ranch—a tradition Heidi and her grandfather had started when they'd first moved to the ranch a couple of years ago. Families drove out for an old-fashioned hayride. The various animals were available for petting, families could take pictures, and if they were very lucky, it might snow.

Evie sort of remembered agreeing to help, but

that was before she'd figured out how busy she was going to be with the production and the other activities someone always seemed to be volunteering her for.

"I wrapped books," she told Annabelle. "Isn't that enough?"

Annabelle raised her chin. "Excuse me, but I'm not in charge of the hayrides. That's Heidi's thing."

"Right," Evie muttered, following her pregnant sister-in-law to-be out of the guest bedroom and toward the rear of the house.

She wanted to complain that she'd had to help everyone. Heidi tonight, Annabelle with the books, her mother with the pet adoption. Only all three of her brothers had shown up to refurbish her production sets, so it wasn't as though she could really complain. And in truth it was kind of fun to be with everyone, in a low-key setting. Still, these were the most intense holidays she could remember.

She stepped out the back door and walked down to the lit pathway. The night was freezing, but clear. So far there wasn't any snow in the forecast. Stars twinkled in the dark sky.

The wagon, decorated with swinging battery-operated lanterns and wreaths, stood by the barn. Shane had already hooked up the horses. Christmas music played from a stereo somewhere, and the scent of hot chocolate drifted on the air. Two cars had already pulled up, and children and adults were spilling out into the hay-riding loading area.

Evie watched them, seeing a familiar blonde woman. She was about to wave to Nevada when she realized the hair was all wrong, as was the man with her. Another of the triplets, she thought. Montana, she remembered.

She walked over. "You came for a hayride."

"How could we resist? I can't believe you have time to be here. Everyone is talking about what you're doing with the dance," Montana said. "We can't wait to see it. This is Simon, my husband, and our daughter, Skye."

Evie glanced down at the baby, prepared to give the obligatory coo. New parents expected that. But as she parted her lips to say something, Skye opened her eyes and stared at her. The baby's mouth was a perfect rosebud shape. The corners turned up as tiny hands clapped together in excitement. Skye giggled and reached for her.

"She likes you," Montana said with a laugh. "She's such a flirt. Would you like to hold her?"

Evie nodded and held out her arms. Montana handed over the happy baby.

Skye was lighter than Evie expected, but warm and smelled sweet. The child held her gaze, still smiling and waving her tiny fingers.

Beyond promising herself that she would never want her child to feel about her the way she felt about May, Evie hadn't thought much about having children. She'd seen marriage and kids as some vague future thing. Someday. Just not now.

But holding Skye made her ache in a way she never had before. She saw possibilities and happiness in the baby's face. Parts of her long dormant stirred to life. She wanted to belong, she realized. She wanted what others considered normal or even traditional. A husband. A family. She no longer wanted to live her life on the outside—watching everyone else be a part of something larger than themselves.

She briefly wondered what Annabelle and Shane's baby would look like and suffered a pang when she realized if she kept to her plan of leaving, she wouldn't be here to see him or her born.

"She's so beautiful," Evie murmured, then passed back the baby.

"I wish I could take credit," Montana said with a laugh. "But she gets her looks from her dad."

"Have fun," Evie told her, then reluctantly walked toward the wagon.

More cars pulled up, and the wagon was loaded. Evie was kept busy posing for pictures with the children and helping people up and down the stairs. When Athena, the most wayward of the goats, made a break for freedom, Evie caught her by her red-and-green collar.

"Not so fast, my pretty," she told the goat. Athena dipped her head and nibbled on Evie's shoe.

They did a steady business. Sometime around eight, she took a break.

"You look great," Dante murmured as he passed her with a tray of clean mugs for the cocoa. "Love the ears. Seriously. Do you get to keep them?"

She grinned. "Having an elf fantasy, are we?"

"The outfit is really working for me."

They were by the back door. Music and laughter surrounded them, but they seemed cut off from the rest of the world. She stared into his eyes and wondered what it would be like to get lost in a guy like Dante. What it would be like to not be afraid to love.

"How are you doing with your family?" he asked. "Too much togetherness?"

"I'm doing okay," she said, pleased she was able to say the words and know they were the truth. "They're growing on me." She grinned. "In a good way." She touched his arm. "Brace yourself."

"I'm braced."

"You were right. About me and my mom."

"Can I get that on a statue of some kind?"

She laughed. "No, but I'm going to say thank you. I'm spending more time with her, and it's not too bad. I'm trying to see things from her perspective. She was young when her husband died. There was a lot on her plate. She could have done better, but no one is perfect."

"Forgiveness?"

"I'm getting there."

"I'm glad." He kissed her lightly. "And later, you, me and the ears?"

She was still laughing when she walked back toward the petting zoo.

"There she is!"

Evie turned toward the familiar voice and spotted her mother walking toward her with an older woman. It took her a second to recognize the mayor.

"This is my daughter, Evie," May was saying. "She's a wonderful dancer. She's taken on *The Dance of the Winter King* by herself, and we're all so proud of her."

Evie felt herself flushing, unaccustomed to the praise. "I'm stepping in to help," she murmured. "I didn't want my students to be disappointed."

"I'm sure they won't be," the mayor told her. "Dominique is thrilled with the work you're doing." The older woman took her hand. "I know you're going to be very happy here in Fool's Gold. You need this town and we need you."

The statement was meant kindly, Evie told herself. Even if it was a little spooky.

"Thank you."

She returned to her elf duties. Heidi gave in to

several pleas from children and brought Priscilla down to the barn for pictures. Evie found herself organizing the line and then taking several of the pictures so the families could all be together by the goats and the elephant and the decorated wagon.

"I want you next to me," a little girl said, then turned to her father. "Daddy, can the girl elf be in the picture?"

Dante moved up next to her and took the camera. "I've got this one," he told her. "Go on. Be a star."

"It's the ears," she told him in a whisper. "Apparently they're irresistible."

He chuckled and waved her into position. She crouched next to the little girl and smiled. After that, Evie found herself posing in several pictures. The evening sped by as more families arrived for their hayride.

A little before nine, the last of the cars drove away. Dante and Shane walked Priscilla back to her custom elephant house while Heidi and Evie carried in trays of mugs to be washed.

"That was fun," Evie admitted as she put a tray on the kitchen counter. "Exhausting but good. How many nights do you have the hayrides?"

She glanced at Heidi and saw her sister-in-law standing with her hand pressed against her stomach, her expression joyful and intense.

"Heidi?" Evie took a step toward her. "Are you all right?"

"I'm fine."

"You look… I don't know. *Strange* isn't the right word. You're not sick, are you?"

"No." Heidi glanced around, as if checking if they were alone, then she turned to Evie. "I shouldn't say anything, but I'm just bursting with the news. Can you keep a secret?"

Normally a statement like that would have had Evie backing out of the room. But Heidi didn't look like the information was going to be scary or upsetting. Instead she was practically glowing with excitement.

"Okay. Sure."

Heidi touched her arm and leaned close. "I'm pregnant," she whispered. "I just got confirmation this morning." Her fingers tightened slightly.

Pregnant? Evie stared at her for a second, then hugged her. "Heidi, that's so wonderful. Congratulations. Rafe doesn't know, does he? He was way too calm for a guy finding out he's going to be a father for the first time."

Heidi grinned. "No and you can't tell him. I'm waiting until Christmas Eve, after the performance. I thought telling him then would be the perfect Christmas present."

"He'll be thrilled," she said. And scared. A

baby. She thought of adorable Skye, whom she'd held earlier, and felt a small ache in her heart.

"I'm just so happy," Heidi told her. "We've talked about starting a family, but it wasn't real to me before. Our child is going to grow up here, on the ranch. In Fool's Gold. I feel so blessed."

Evie knew that Heidi had gone through a lot to end up where she was today. The blessings had been earned the hard way. But in the end, she'd had her happy ending. Evie wondered if anyone could find one or if they were reserved for a special few.

Shane strolled into the kitchen, ending any chance to continue the conversation. Evie went outside. She saw Dante leading a very reluctant Athena toward the goat barn.

"You have to go inside," he told the animal. "It's cold outside. You need to be warm."

Athena made a grumbling noise in her throat.

"Fine," Dante told her with a sigh. "Here."

He handed over a piece of carrot. The goat took it and then followed dutifully as he went inside.

She thought about how Dante had been so patient with the children and how he'd teased her about her elf ears. As she'd known for a while, he was one of the good ones.

He stepped out of the goat barn and carefully closed the door, then spotted her and waved. Moonlight touched his face, illuminated the handsome lines, while his broad shoulders cast a shadow on the frozen ground. She thought of the baby she'd held and the longing in her heart, and then she knew.

She'd fallen in love with Dante.

She wasn't supposed to have given her heart. In fact, she would have sworn she was immune to that kind of thing. He'd made it clear he wasn't interested in any kind of long-term relationship, that he didn't do love or forever. He wouldn't risk those kinds of feelings. She knew she'd never been in love before. Not really.

So how had this happened? Was it because of everything else going on? Had she been so caught up in the performance and the town and fitting in that she'd forgotten to protect her heart? Or was it simply that Dante was the one? The one man in the world who was everything she'd ever wanted, and once she met him, falling had been inevitable?

Either way, she was in love with him. A reality that both excited and terrified her. Because she had no idea what she was supposed to do now.

Fifteen

"I'M REALLY MORE a dog person," May said with a sigh. "I hope the cats couldn't tell."

Evie put the last of the brushes and combs on the towel to dry. "You were very affectionate with the cats," she told her mother. "I don't think they had their feelings hurt."

May raised her eyebrows. "Are you mocking me?"

"A little."

"I see." She smiled. "Fine. I suppose it's a silly thing to say. Worrying that the cats will know they're not my favorite."

"Imagine how the fish feel."

They'd just spent an afternoon grooming pets for the upcoming adoption. The adoption was in two days. After that, it was a fast ten days until the performance. Then she could rest. But between then and now was enough work to keep fifteen elves busy.

They collected their coats and walked outside. It was nearly five and already dark.

May looked at her. "Don't you have dance classes today? Did I make you cancel them?"

"No. The school holiday programs are all today, so there weren't any lessons scheduled. That's why I asked if we could do the grooming today instead of tomorrow. Starting on Monday, we get access to the high school's auditorium, and we all get to practice on the actual stage. That will be fun."

And cause for panic, she thought, wondering if she really could pull the show together in time. A problem for tomorrow, she told herself.

"Want to get some dinner?" May asked, her voice suddenly tentative.

Evie was tired and ready for a few hours of quiet, but somehow she found herself wanting to spend more time with her mother. After taking Dante's advice and accepting her share of the responsibility for their continued estrangement, she found herself a little more open to the thought of family.

"Sure," she said.

They discussed options and ended up deciding on Angelo's for Italian food.

They drove into town and found parking behind the restaurant. The whitewashed building had been draped in colored lights that glowed against the pale background. In the spring and summer, a big patio provided outdoor seating, but in the middle of winter, the tables and chairs had been put away. A Christmas tree took their place.

They walked inside and were shown to a quiet booth by the front windows. After glancing over the menu, May looked at Evie.

"Thanks for helping with the hayrides," she said. "I think everyone had a good time."

"They did," Evie agreed. "The kids loved having a chance to pet Priscilla."

"She's very good with children. I think she's happy, all settled with her new herd."

Evie wasn't sure Priscilla would consider a pony and a pig much of a herd, but they were company.

Their server appeared, and they each ordered a glass of wine and the house lasagna. For once Evie wasn't going to sweat the calories. She'd been dancing a lot, and if she had to deal with an extra few pounds after Christmas, then just like much of America, she would make a resolution to lose weight.

"Are you happy with your townhouse?" May asked.

"It works for me," Evie said. "The location is good. I can walk to work, which is kind of fun. I'm sure saving on gas."

May offered her a piece of bread from the basket, which Evie refused, then took one for herself. "You're renting, aren't you? I was wondering if you'd thought of maybe buying something." Her mother picked up the small ceramic container of butter, then put it back down. She glanced at the table, then the bread, then back at Evie. "I would like to help with the down payment. If you plan to stay. In town, I mean."

Evie stared at her mother, confused about the entire conversation until she realized that May was nervous. About the offer and maybe the question of whether or not Evie was planning on staying in Fool's Gold.

As little as two weeks ago, Evie would have announced she was leaving as soon as she had a year's worth of experience. That would have given her enough time to save enough money to relocate. But since talking to Dominique, she was less sure about her plans. Her boss's suggestions for the business were exciting, and the idea of being a partner thrilled her. There was also the unexpected tug of family.

The server appeared with their wine and their salads. Evie waited until she was gone, then drew in a breath.

"I'm not sure what I'm going to do," she admitted. "Whether I want to buy or not. But I appreciate your offer. It's very generous."

Her mother studied her anxiously. "So you might be staying?"

Evie smiled. "Yes. I think I might."

May relaxed against the back of the booth. "That's good to hear. I had hoped you would like it here. Everyone is so welcoming. The town has an interesting history. You should get Annabelle to tell you about the women who first came here. They're from the Máa-zib tribe. Very matriarchal. It's fascinating." May frowned. "Hmm, didn't the Mayans predict the world is going to end soon? Sometime this year?"

"If it is, it had better hurry," Evie said, stabbing a piece of lettuce with her fork. "The year is nearly over. And if anyone is listening, I would really appreciate being able to get through *The Dance of the Winter King* before the world ends. My girls have worked hard and deserve their chance to shine."

May raised her wineglass. "We'll toast the girls."

They sipped their wine. Evie gave in to temptation and took a piece of bread, then put a little butter on her plate. She'd just taken her first, amazingly delicious bite when her mother asked, "How are things going with Dante?"

Fortunately Evie hadn't started swallowing yet, so she was able to compose herself and not choke. But chewing and swallowing only took so long, and then she was still left with a question she didn't know how to answer. Despite her tentative peace with her mother, she wasn't ready to announce she'd fallen in love with a man who didn't want to love her back.

"We're doing well," she said instead. "He's a good guy."

"So Rafe tells me. Although he does have a bit of a reputation with women."

"Dante made it clear from the start that he doesn't do long-term relationships." She couldn't fault him for leading her on.

"You're all right with that?"

"I wasn't looking for a relationship at all," she admitted. "This whole thing started with us getting each other through the holidays. Now it's more than that. We like each other." Which was the truth. After all, she did like him. She also loved him, but she wasn't ready to talk about that yet.

"Tell me about the other men in your life."

Evie wrinkled her nose. "There's not much to tell. I've dated some good guys and some not-so-good guys, but I haven't ever fallen in love. I guess I haven't met the one." Until now, she thought with a sigh. But why go there?

Her mother nodded slowly, as if not surprised. "I'm responsible for that."

"Mom, I'm willing to put a lot on you, but I don't think you get the blame for my sucky love life."

"You were afraid to find someone you could love because you didn't want to be hurt again. Rejected. I would guess you're afraid to love someone because you're convinced he won't love you back."

Evie opened her mouth, then closed it. May's words had a ring of truth. "I have been afraid to give my heart," she admitted slowly.

May blinked several times, as if fighting tears. "I'm so sorry."

"Don't apologize. I picked the guys. Not you."

"But if I'd been there for you…" May held up her hand. "I'll stop now. I want us to have a nice dinner. I've said what I wanted to say and apologized. You can think about it, and we'll deal with it again another time. How's that?"

"I can live with that."

"Good."

They talked about the costumes for the performance. Evie had seen a few of them, although not all. They were scattered around town, being altered and redone by an assortment of volunteers.

"I'm looking forward to comparing this year's dances with what was done in previous years," she said. "I asked Clay to record the whole thing for me."

"You know we're all coming," May said. "I've already bought my tickets."

"I hope you enjoy it."

"I will. When you were little, I loved to watch you dance."

Their server appeared with their entrées. When she'd left, May leaned toward Evie.

"Why did you leave Juilliard? Do you mind telling me? I never understood your decision."

Evie shrugged. "I wasn't good enough. After six months, I was called into the office and told I didn't have the talent. I worked hard, but without the raw ability, I couldn't achieve their standards. Rather than wait until they forced me to leave, I quit."

May's eyes widened. "I can't believe that. You're a wonderful dancer."

"You're not a professional. Trust me, I'm no Dominique Guérin." She thought about being only a few weeks from her eighteenth birthday and knowing she was all alone in the world. She'd had nothing but a shattered dream and the blistered and callused feet of a dancer.

"I wish you'd come home," her mother whispered. "I wish I'd told you I wanted you to come home."

"Neither of us were ready then, Mom," Evie said. "We needed time. I needed to grow up."

"I think I did, too. I missed so much. I'm such a fool."

"You're a good person. You just got a little sideways."

"You're being generous with me. I don't deserve it."

"I think I get to decide that. Not you."

Evie waited for the anger to reemerge, but there was only lingering sadness and a growing sense of peace. Yes, May had made mistakes. She'd been thoughtless. But she'd also had stresses and responsibilities. Evie realized she could spend the rest of her life hating her mother. But to what end? She would only end up bitter and alone. May had acknowledged what she'd done wrong and tried to make amends. Wasn't it better to forgive and take what was offered?

"Is that lasagna?"

Evie looked up and saw Clay standing by the table, his gaze on her plate. She sighed.

"Is Charlie working?"

"Uh-huh. Move over, kid."

She did as he asked, and he slid in next to her.

"Hi, Mom," he said as he reached for the bread with one hand and her fork with another. "You weren't going to eat this, were you?"

"Apparently not."

"Good. I'm starving. So what are you two talking about?"

Evie flagged the server, knowing she would have to order another entrée if she expected to eat. Then she smiled at her mother and said, "Girl stuff. Just girl stuff."

"HE DID NOT," Charlie said as she dumped chocolate chips into a bowl.

"I swear." Evie made an X on her chest. She'd just told Charlie about Clay showing up at the restaurant and eating her dinner.

"I'm going to have a serious talk with him," Charlie promised. "He can't do that."

"He misses you when you're working," Heidi said, stirring butter in a second bowl. Evie wasn't sure, but thought she might be making peanut-butter cookies.

Annabelle handed two eggs to Heidi. "She's right. I mean, I would have attacked him if he'd tried to take food from me, but he got lonely. Like a little puppy."

"A puppy who needs some training," Charlie grumbled.

Evie grinned.

The four of them were in Shane and Annabelle's new house, making Christmas cookies. Evie had gotten the call the previous evening for a Sunday afternoon bake-fest. Just the four "sisters," Annabelle had said. While she had a million things she needed to be doing, she'd found herself saying she would be there.

Now cooling racks overflowed with cookies. By the time these last batches were done, the sugar cookies would be room temperature and ready for frosting.

"When I was a kid," Heidi said, breaking the eggs over the bowl, "Christmas was a big deal. We had our extended, carnival family and planned out who would cook what. Someone took the turkey, someone else the potatoes and so on."

"My holidays were quiet," Annabelle said. "When my parents were together, they were fighting, and after they were divorced, they traveled." She smiled. "Don't feel bad. I liked when they were gone. I spent the holidays with my friends, and their parents felt sorry for me, so they went out of their way to make me feel welcome. It was like being a visiting princess."

"I liked the holidays," Charlie told them. "Especially when my mom was away performing. Then it was my dad and me."

"So we're all dysfunctional," Evie said, keeping her tone light. "Except for Heidi."

"Yes, but not to worry." Charlie grinned. "No one likes her."

"Cheap talk." Heidi stirred the peanut butter into her cookie batter. "I know you all love me."

As far as Evie could tell, no one else knew about Heidi's pregnancy. She really was keeping it a secret until Christmas Eve when she told Rafe. Evie wasn't sure why she'd been Heidi's confidant, but she had to admit she liked knowing about the tiny life growing inside of her sister-in-law.

"What was Shane like when he was a kid?" Annabelle asked. "Any embarrassing stories you want to share? Something I can torture him with later?"

"He was in a band," Evie told her. "When we moved to L.A. For about six months."

"A band?" Annabelle leaned against the counter and sighed. "You've just given me the best gift ever. Did he sing?"

"I think he played bass and maybe sang backup."

Charlie and Heidi both stared at her, their expressions expectant.

"And?" Charlie prodded.

Evie tried to remember what her brothers had done when they'd been younger. "Clay dressed up like Dorothy from *The Wizard of Oz* one Halloween and Rafe crashed his best friend's car the same day his friend got it as a gift."

Heidi's eyes widened in horror.

"It wasn't a bad accident," Evie added quickly. "Just a fender bender. Actually I think it was the fender that had to be replaced."

"Thank goodness," Heidi said. "If it was serious, I couldn't tease him about it."

"He was humiliated, not hurt," Evie assured her.

While they'd been talking, Charlie had finished mixing the chocolate chip cookies and was putting spoonfuls onto a cookie sheet. When she turned to put the trays into the oven, Annabelle picked up the spoon.

"I'm not supposed to eat raw cookie dough, right?" she asked. "It's the eggs."

Charlie pushed the cookie sheet onto the oven rack, closed the door and straightened, then grabbed the spoon from Annabelle's hand.

"No, you're not supposed to eat that." She held up the bag of chocolate chips and shook it. A few rattled inside. "I saved you some."

Annabelle smiled, then sniffed. "You're so good to me."

"I swear, if you cry, I'll…"

"Yes? You'll what? Hit me? Hit a pregnant woman? I don't think so."

"You're so smug."

"I know. It's not as good as being tall like you, but I'll take it."

"They're always like this," Heidi told Evie. "They squabble and then they make up. I think it's because they're total opposites and yet completely alike."

"That's not possible," Charlie said.

Evie studied the two of them. "I see what you mean."

Heidi handed her a fork to start making the cross marks on the peanut butter cookies.

This time last year, Evie had been in Los Angeles, in her tiny apartment, working as a waitress and spending her Sundays as an L.A. Stallions cheerleader. She'd been pretty much on her own, with only a few friends she could depend on. This year everything was different. She was with her family, had new friends and was crazy in love.

Sure there were complications, but she had to admit, when comparing the two scenarios, her life had taken a turn for the better. The much better.

Sixteen

EVIE STOOD ON the stage in the high school auditorium and looked out at the rows of empty seats. With the upper-level seating, there were nearly eight hundred seats. That was a huge intimidation factor for her students, which was one of the reasons all their practices were now going to be here. They had to get used to the bigger stage and the—

Her cell phone rang.

"Hello?"

"It's Gideon. Where are you?"

Evie frowned and glanced around at the empty auditorium. She and Gideon had a noon meeting to discuss the changes he wanted to make in the voice-over for the show. He was late. "I'm at the high school. Where are you?"

"At the convention center. The sound system sucks, by the way. I've already put a call into Mayor Marsha. She said I can bring in any equipment I like." He chuckled. "She has no idea what she's agreed to."

"Why are you at the convention center?"

"Because that's where the performance is."

Evie's stomach contracted. "No. It's at the high school."

"It *was* at the high school. But there isn't enough seating. This was all decided months ago. Didn't anyone tell you?"

"No." She had a feeling Miss Monica knew, but that was just one more detail the dance instructor hadn't shared when she'd run off with her gentleman friend. "Wait. The adoption is there. How will there be room?"

"It's a big convention center," Gideon told her. "There's room."

She promised to hurry and raced to her car. It only took a few minutes to drive to the convention center. As she waited at one of the few stoplights in town, she tried to recall the conversations she'd had with her students. Now that she thought about it, she'd always talked about the stage. She'd meant the one at the high school but hadn't been specific. No wonder no one had corrected her. They hadn't known she was wrong.

She pulled into the convention center parking lot and stopped at the entrance that had a large pickup truck in front of it. It looked like the sort

SUSAN MALLERY

77778	THREE LITTLE WORDS	___ $7.99 U.S.	___ $8.99 CAN.
77768	TWO OF A KIND	___ $7.99 U.S.	___ $9.99 CAN.
77760	JUST ONE KISS	___ $7.99 U.S.	___ $9.99 CAN.
77694	ALL SUMMER LONG	___ $7.99 U.S.	___ $9.99 CAN.
77687	SUMMER NIGHTS	___ $7.99 U.S.	___ $9.99 CAN.
77683	SUMMER DAYS	___ $7.99 U.S.	___ $9.99 CAN.
77594	ONLY YOURS	___ $7.99 U.S.	___ $9.99 CAN.
77588	ONLY MINE	___ $7.99 U.S.	___ $9.99 CAN.
77533	SWEET TROUBLE	___ $7.99 U.S.	___ $9.99 CAN.
77531	SWEET SPOT	___ $7.99 U.S.	___ $9.99 CAN.
77529	FALLING FOR GRACIE	___ $7.99 U.S.	___ $9.99 CAN.
77527	ACCIDENTALLY YOURS	___ $7.99 U.S.	___ $9.99 CAN.
77519	SIZZLING	___ $7.99 U.S.	___ $9.99 CAN.
77510	IRRESISTIBLE	___ $7.99 U.S.	___ $9.99 CAN.
77490	ALMOST PERFECT	___ $7.99 U.S.	___ $9.99 CAN.
77468	FINDING PERFECT	___ $7.99 U.S.	___ $9.99 CAN.
77465	SOMEONE LIKE YOU	___ $7.99 U.S.	___ $9.99 CAN.
77452	CHASING PERFECT	___ $7.99 U.S.	___ $9.99 CAN.
77384	HOT ON HER HEELS	___ $7.99 U.S.	___ $9.99 CAN.
77372	LIP SERVICE	___ $7.99 U.S.	___ $8.99 CAN.

(limited quantities available)

TOTAL AMOUNT $ _____
POSTAGE & HANDLING $ _____
($1.00 FOR 1 BOOK, 50¢ for each additional)
APPLICABLE TAXES* $ _____
TOTAL PAYABLE $ _____

(check or money order—please do not send cash)

To order, complete this form and send it, along with a check or money order for the total above, payable to Harlequin HQN, to: **In the U.S.:** 3010 Walden Avenue, P.O. Box 9077, Buffalo, NY 14269-9077; **In Canada:** P.O. Box 636, Fort Erie, Ontario, L2A 5X3.

Name: _____
Address: _____ City: _____
State/Prov.: _____ Zip/Postal Code: _____
Account Number (if applicable): _____
075 CSAS

*New York residents remit applicable sales taxes.
*Canadian residents remit applicable GST and provincial taxes.

HARLEQUIN® HQN™
www.Harlequin.com

PHSM1113BL

A fun, unexpected and totally addictive story from
New York Times **bestselling author**

KRISTAN HIGGINS

After being unceremoniously rejected by her lifelong crush, Honor Holland is going to pick herself up, dust herself off and get back out there.... Or she would if dating in Manningsport, New York, population 715, wasn't easier said than done. And charming, handsome British professor Tom Barlow comes with complications. He just wants to do right by his unofficial stepson, Charlie, but his visa is about to expire. Now Tom must either get a green card or leave the States—and leave Charlie behind.

In a moment of impulsiveness, Honor agrees to help Tom with a marriage of convenience—and make her ex jealous in the process. As sparks start to fly between Honor and Tom, they might discover that their pretend relationship is far too perfect to be anything but true love....

> "Kristan Higgins not only knows how to write the woo, she knows how to show her reader a good time."
> —*USA TODAY*

Be sure to connect with us at:

Harlequin.com/Newsletters
Facebook.com/HarlequinBooks
Twitter.com/HarlequinBooks

REQUEST YOUR
FREE BOOKS!

2 FREE NOVELS
FROM THE ROMANCE COLLECTION
PLUS 2 FREE GIFTS!

YES! Please send me 2 FREE novels from the Romance Collection and my 2 FREE gifts (gifts are worth about $10). After receiving them, if I don't wish to receive any more books, I can return the shipping statement marked "cancel." If I don't cancel, I will receive 4 brand-new novels every month and be billed just $6.24 per book in the U.S. or $6.74 per book in Canada. That's a savings of at least 22% off the cover price. It's quite a bargain! Shipping and handling is just 50¢ per book in the U.S. and 75¢ per book in Canada.* I understand that accepting the 2 free books and gifts places me under no obligation to buy anything. I can always return a shipment and cancel at any time. Even if I never buy another book, the two free books and gifts are mine to keep forever.

194/394 MDN F4XY

Name	(PLEASE PRINT)	
Address		Apt. #
City	State/Prov.	Zip/Postal Code

Signature (if under 18, a parent or guardian must sign)

Mail to the Harlequin® Reader Service:
IN U.S.A.: P.O. Box 1867, Buffalo, NY 14240-1867
IN CANADA: P.O. Box 609, Fort Erie, Ontario L2A 5X3

Want to try two free books from another line?
Call 1-800-873-8635 or visit www.ReaderService.com.

There's nowhere better to spend the holidays than with *New York Times* bestselling author

SUSAN MALLERY

in the town of Fool's Gold, where love is always waiting to be unwrapped...

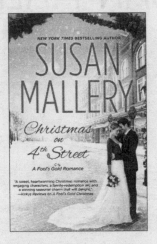

Available now wherever books are sold!

"Susan Mallery is one of my favorites."
—#1 *New York Times* bestselling author Debbie Macomber

www.SusanMallery.com

of vehicle Gideon would drive. She grabbed her bag and paperwork and raced inside.

Sure enough, a big stage had been set up, and there were rows and rows of chairs.

"Oh, no," she said, coming to a stop and staring at the empty seats. "There has to be room for at least a couple of thousand people."

"Three thousand, two hundred," Gideon said, strolling up to greet her. "Mayor Marsha is convinced the program is going to be a success."

"That's too many people. My girls will freak. I would freak if it were me."

"They'll be fine."

"Easy for you to say. You're not the one doing the dances."

She was still trying to process the change in venue. All this time she'd had the high school auditorium in her head. Why had no one mentioned the convention center?

"Look at it this way," Gideon said with a wink. "At least you won't have far to go after the pet adoption."

"I'm going to throw up."

Gideon held up both hands and took a step back. "No reason for that to happen. Take a deep breath. In for the count of four, hold for the count of four, exhale for the count of four."

She stared at him. "Excuse me?"

"It's a breathing exercise. You work up to a count of ten or twelve, but that takes practice."

"Seriously?"

Gideon surprised her by winking. "I have mysterious depths."

"Apparently."

He was casually dressed in jeans and a long-sleeved plaid shirt, the sleeves rolled up to his elbows. She studied the part of the tattoo visible on his forearm and then looked into his dark, unreadable eyes. She could imagine Gideon doing a lot of things. Holding a gun, giving orders, riding a motorcycle, but she couldn't picture him on a yoga mat practicing his breathing.

"Ex-military?" she asked.

"Maybe."

Despite the three thousand, two hundred empty seats and the incredible list of things she had to get through between this moment and the performance, she laughed. "Because if you told me, you'd have to kill me?"

"Something like that." He shrugged. "I've been places and done things. One day I decided I was done. When my tour ended I went looking for a way to make peace. With myself, at least, and maybe the world. I ended up in a shack in Bali."

"Bali? Not Tibet?"

"I'm more a beach guy."

"Nice work if you can get it."

"There was a teacher there. He taught me—"

For a second something flashed through Gideon's eyes. Evie couldn't say what it was, but she would swear there was pain involved. Something cold and ugly that made her shiver. Then he blinked and it was gone.

"He taught me how to keep on moving forward," Gideon continued. "When I left, I remembered a buddy of mine talking about this place. He grew up here, and when he talked about home, he made it sound like the only place worth living."

"Who was the guy?"

"Ford Hendrix."

"Oh. I know who he is. Well, not him, but his sisters." She laughed. "Did he also tell you that living in this town is like trying to put a puzzle together? I wonder if I'll ever get all the names straight. But I think my mom knows his mom. But he's not here."

"He's still serving. He'll be back soon."

She thought about asking "back from where," but reality returned in the form of all those empty chairs and a ball of panic bouncing off the walls of her stomach.

"Did I already mention I think I'm going to throw up?"

"Yes, but now I don't believe you."

"Fine. Risk your shoes. See if I care." She shook her head. "Okay. I'm focusing. The changes in the

script for the narration are great. I love them." She pulled several sheets of paper out of her handbag and shuffled through them. "I want to make sure we're on target with the transitions of the dancers. I've marked this copy with where I think the girls will be moving on and off the stage."

He moved close and studied the pages. "Sure. I see what you're doing. So you want me to pause until everyone is off stage before starting?"

"Right." She glanced up at him. "You're coming to the dress rehearsal, aren't you?"

He nodded. "Give me your schedule. I'll get to at least one other before then, so we can do a run-through from the top."

"That would be great."

DANTE WALKED INTO THE convention center, still not sure why he'd been summoned. Mayor Marsha had called and gone on about a large space and the sound system. Just when he'd started wondering how he was going to politely get her off the phone, she'd asked him to meet Evie right away. He'd agreed, grateful to be able to hang up.

Now he watched her up on stage, standing close to Gideon, their heads bent over sheets of paper. Evie pointed to something and Gideon nodded. His arm brushed hers as he took another paper and held it close to the first.

His head knew there was nothing between

them. That Evie spent most nights in his bed, or he in hers. While neither of them was looking for a serious kind of relationship, they were, in the confines of what they had, monogamous. He'd considered himself civilized for many years now. Law-abiding. He was a lawyer, which made him, by definition, boring.

But deep inside, something stirred. Something heavy and ugly that wanted to propel him to the stage. He didn't just want to step between them, he wanted to push Gideon away. He wanted to hurt the other man and then stand over his broken body and pound his chest as a sign of victory.

The flush of intense emotion faded as quickly as it had risen, but the remnants left him shaken. What the hell was he thinking? Beat up some guy and then do a victory dance? What was he, seventeen again? Mature, sensible people didn't act like that. *He* didn't act like that.

Evie said something he couldn't hear, and Gideon walked away. A couple of seconds later, music filled the open space.

"That's it," Evie called and put down the papers. She shrugged out of her coat, revealing body-hugging dance clothes. As always, the sight of her body in all its perfection moved blood from his head to points farther south.

Then she began to dance.

She moved across the stage. She was strong and

elegant at the same time. Lithe, graceful. He could watch her forever.

Behind him, he heard quiet conversation. He turned and saw several of her students had walked in. They were dressed exactly like her—in black tights and black leotards. Their hair was in braids wrapped around their heads, just like her.

The girls, ranging in age from maybe seven to twelve, didn't notice him. They only saw Evie. A couple of them held out their arms, as if dancing with her. He heard whispers of "Beautiful" and "Oh, look at that turn."

They wanted to be just like her.

He knew Evie had been brought to Fool's Gold under difficult circumstances. The last thing she'd been looking for was a connection with her family. But she'd found that, along with a place to belong. He would guess her plans to leave in a few months were also unraveling. Fool's Gold was now home.

He was a man who had gone out of his way never to form serious connections. Oh, sure, he was friends with Rafe, but that was different. Caring about a woman meant risking more than he was willing to put on the line.

But what if Evie needed him to care now? Everything in her life was coming together. It would only be natural for her to start looking at the future. If her needs had changed, then he needed to back off. To make sure she wasn't expecting more

than he could give. Only he wasn't ready to stop seeing her. He *liked* seeing her.

The music ended, and the girls clapped. Evie turned toward the sound and smiled when she saw her students. Then her gaze met his, and the smile became a little wicked.

He grinned in return.

Maybe he was reading too much into the situation, he told himself. Just because she was finding her way with her family and enjoying the town didn't mean she wanted more from him. He would wait and watch. If things seemed different between them, then he would act. Until then, he would hang on and enjoy the ride.

"DO YOU HAVE any idea how many seats that is?" Evie asked, sitting up and reaching for her glass of wine.

"Three thousand, two hundred?" Dante asked.

She turned to him. "I'm seriously on the edge. Don't mess with me."

He leaned in and kissed her. "You don't scare me. I used to be bad."

They were at his place, curled up together in the living room. The gas fireplace flickered away. After an afternoon of practicing with her students on the huge stage at the convention center, Evie was both exhausted and wired.

His mouth lingered, causing her to relax. This

was nice, she thought. Spending time with him, touching him, being touched. Except for her being in love and him not in love with her, it was about as close to perfect as she'd ever gotten.

He drew back and she sighed.

"I feel so stupid."

"It's an honest mistake. Everyone thought you already knew and you didn't."

"I know." She scooted back into the arm of the sofa and rested her sock-covered feet on his lap. "But I'm still playing catch-up. That place is huge."

"Your girls will be fine. You've done a great job with them."

"They're the ones who worked hard." She drew in a breath. "But it's done. We're there and we're practicing, and I'll be fine. I hope."

He rested his hand on her legs. "You'll be fine." He leaned to the side and pulled a flat package out of the drawer of the end table, then handed it to her. "This will distract you."

She stared at the simply wrapped package. "You bought me a gift."

"It's not a Christmas present. Don't freak out."

"I'm not freaking, and it is wrapped in Christmas paper."

"They offered, I said yes. Like I told you, it's no big deal."

Except it was a big deal to her. Dante had bought her something.

She took the package and realized it was a book. After carefully opening it, she stared at the cover. *Cats for Dummies.*

She looked at him.

"You're thinking of getting that cat," he told her. "I saw this and thought it would help you decide."

Love flooded her and it was all she could do to hold in the words. She settled on throwing herself at him and hugging him.

"Thank you," she murmured.

"You're welcome." He wrapped his arms around her. "This is nice. I didn't know you responded so well to presents. I'll have to remember that."

"Knock, knock."

Dante looked up from his computer and saw May walking toward his desk. It was lunchtime and nearly everyone was gone. Something about a holiday get-together, he thought. Or maybe not. He'd been busy with a new construction contract and not paying attention.

Now he resurfaced long enough to stand and greet his partner's mother.

"Am I interrupting?" May asked. "Silly question. You're focused on something."

"I could use a break." He motioned to the chair by his desk. "Can I get you a cup of coffee?"

"I'm fine." May waved him back to his seat.

"Sit. I'll only be here for a second. I want to ask you something."

She probably wanted gift suggestions for Rafe, Dante thought as he settled back in his chair. He was a guy. He didn't know what Rafe wanted.

"I wanted to thank you," May said. "For helping me with Evie." She smiled at him. "I know you encouraged her to give me a chance, and I'm very grateful."

He wasn't comfortable with praise. "I pointed out that it takes two to fight and asked if that's what she wanted for her relationship with her family."

"You're being modest, which I happen to know isn't like you." She stared into his eyes. "You encouraged her to have an open mind. That allowed her to consider I might be telling the truth when I apologized for all I'd done."

She dropped her gaze to her hands and twisted her fingers together. "I was so wrong and so horrible. I'm still wrestling with how I acted. Evie is being so generous in letting me be a part of her life again. I'm getting a second chance and I'm grateful."

"Ah, good." Dante shifted on his seat and hoped they were done talking about emotions. The only way this could get worse was for May to start crying.

Rafe's mother glanced back at him. "That's why I'm worried about your relationship with her."

Dante realized he'd been wrong. Tears weren't the only way this could get worse.

"You're a good man," she continued. "Rafe speaks highly of you, and I respect his opinion. But he's also said you're not someone interested in a long-term relationship." She stared at him, her eyes pleading. "I just got my daughter back. I don't want her hurt."

He swore silently, wishing he were anywhere but here. "I appreciate your concern, and I share it. I don't want Evie hurt, either. We're both clear on what's going on. We've talked about it."

May's expression softened, and the tension left her shoulders. "You have? Oh, that's a relief. Rafe didn't tell me that. I was afraid…" She shrugged. "It doesn't matter. As long as the two of you are clear on the ground rules. Evie has a good head on her shoulders."

"I agree. We both know this is just for fun." He was careful not to mention the sex. That would only send the conversation back to disaster.

"At the risk of sounding eighty years old," May said with a smile, "I don't understand you young people today. I could never get as involved with a man as Evie is with you and not fall in love. I'm not built that way. Of course, I never expected to

ever fall in love again, and look what happened to me. I'm a newlywed. And at my age."

Still smiling, she rose. "Thanks so much for taking the time to speak with me. I know you're busy. We'll be seeing you for Christmas dinner, won't we?"

Dante stood and nodded automatically, but his attention was elsewhere. May's words repeated themselves over and over in his brain, getting louder with each iteration.

"I could never get as involved with a man as Evie is with you and not fall in love."

He was aware of walking May to the door and saying he would see her tomorrow, at the pet adoption. Somehow he made his way back to his desk and settled in his chair. But he didn't bother looking at his computer. After all, he wouldn't really see it.

There were rules, he reminded himself. They'd both been clear. Neither of them would get emotionally involved. But he'd been jealous of Evie when he'd seen her with Gideon. Jealousy meant he cared about her more than he should. What was the next step? Buying spontaneous presents? Looking forward to seeing her and spending time with her? Imagining a future with her?

No. No way in hell. He didn't fall for anyone. He wasn't that guy. He didn't do love.

He'd learned that lesson a long time ago and he

was never going back. Not for anyone. Now the only question was what to do to fix the situation without anyone getting hurt.

Seventeen

"IT'S COMPLICATED," PATIENCE said.

"But they're sisters." Evie glanced at the two fortysomething salon owners, standing on opposite sides of the stage at the convention center. "And they both do hair."

"Yes, but they have competing salons and they rarely speak. It's all very mysterious. No one knows exactly why they're estranged. A few times a year, they show up at the same event. And they've always helped out with *The Dance of the Winter King*. Don't worry. They'll be fine."

"They'd better be, because I can't take on one more thing." Evie eyed the two women, then figured it wasn't her rock to carry. Besides, when it came to family, she was hardly in a position to be critical.

Today was reserved for costume fittings and hair and makeup consults. In front of the stage about ten women sat with pins and tape measures

and stacks of costumes. The girls were to show up at a specific time, in groups, so they could try on their costumes all at once. Then they would have their time with the stylists. Evie was already on her second latte and assumed there would be a third.

There was a planned break between twelve and one. Charlie had called the previous night to inform her that the Fox and Hound and Jo's Bar had joined together to donate lunch for the volunteers. But before they got to resting, they had to work.

Fortunately for her, everyone else participating had done this before. The girls were quickly ushered into a makeshift dressing area and sorted by size. The first costumes were handed out. Evie waited anxiously for the parade of seven- and eight-year-old girls in pink leotards and tights with silver tutus and angel wings.

"Bring them over here first," Denise Hendrix told her. "Every year those wings need to be anchored. We don't want any of the angels to have a costume malfunction."

Evie ushered each of the girls to a seamstress who made sure the costume fit perfectly and that the wings were secure. After the girls changed back into their regular clothes, Evie led them to the "hair and makeup" station, on the big stage.

"We want to look like Evie," Lillie told her mom. "With our hair in braids."

Patience smiled. "I think that's a great idea.

With the wings, you'll want your hair out of the way."

She turned to Bella and Julia. "How about silver and pink ribbons woven through their hair?"

Bella, or maybe Julia, nodded. "That would be pretty. Now for the fun stuff."

The girls crowded around the trays of eye shadow and lip glosses. Evie glanced over their heads and realized the colors were bright and glittery. No subtle nudes for her girls. The two sisters tried different glosses on the girls' lips and took the time to discuss options with each of them.

"This is really fun," Evie told Patience.

Her friend laughed. "I know. For me it's nearly as great as the performance itself." She lowered her voice. "On the younger girls, we keep it simple. The eye shadow and lip gloss. We don't put mascara on them until they're older. Still, for most of them, this is really special. The costumes and stage makeup add to the thrill."

Evie noticed that each of the girls was given a few minutes to make her selections, that no one was rushed and that both sisters made a point of encouraging the girls to enjoy being the center of attention.

Her next group arrived right on time. They were her tap girls and would wear red sequined outfits with a tuxedo influence. They also had hats and canes they'd been using as props. But the ones in

the studio were old and battered while the canes they would use in the performance nearly blinded with shiny glitter.

And so it went, with group after group moving through hair and makeup. Just before lunch Annabelle and Heidi showed up with the food and drinks. Mayor Marsha made an appearance, along with several of the city council members. By three everyone had been fitted and prepped.

Evie was the last to leave. She walked to the stage and turned to stare at the waiting chairs. Yes, there would be a large audience, but she knew her dancers would be fine. They had practiced and were excited, and this was going to be the best *Dance of the Winter King* ever.

She already had ideas for next year's performance and was excited about starting a toddler dance class. Dominique had said a second time that she wanted to take Evie on as a partner. Everything she'd ever been looking for was right here.

Evie walked to her car. Tomorrow was the pet adoption, which meant a morning of setting up and then the actual event. Three days later she'd help stage the first full-on rehearsal. So far each of the groups had danced at the event center but none of them had gone through the entire show together. In a week, they would have the dress rehearsal and then the performance itself on Christmas Eve.

A busy but satisfying schedule, she thought.

So she really needed to get home and get to bed early. But instead of driving to her townhouse, Evie found herself pulling into the parking lot of the local pet store. Today had shown her where she belonged. That meant it was time for her to take the next step in building a home—adopting Alexander.

She went inside and grabbed a cart, then headed for the cat section. She found litter, a cat box and scooper, food and water dishes, a bed and a few toys. She also picked up a soft cat brush and a blue picture frame with a paw-print and the word Meow in the corner.

As she waited to pay, she made a quick call to the shelter and asked Tammy to put a hold on the cat. She would fill out the adoption paperwork in the morning and make it official. It might take some doing, but she was determined to show Alexander that he could trust her to always be there for him.

"IF THE PET ADOPTION is here," Dante said, straightening the table. "Why are there booths in the center of town?"

"It's the annual Day of Giving," Evie told him. "I'm not sure exactly what that means. What I heard is various charities are here to talk about what they do so people can make donations and

get involved. That finishes at one, and then the pet adoption starts."

They were nearly done setting up for the adoption. The open area they were using was at the far end of the convention center, away from the stage. There was a section for cats, another for dogs and a third area for all other pets. There was a large cage for the kittens to play in and a puppy pen. Tables would hold the cages for the cats, while most of the dogs would be on leashes. Local teens helped with the event, each taking a dog and making sure he or she stayed calm and friendly. The teens also took the dogs outside regularly to mitigate any accidents.

May and Tammy, along with several shelter volunteers, had left to start caravanning the animals from the shelter to the convention center.

"My mom said last year all the animals were adopted. Even an iguana. That's a lot of pressure."

"You'll be fine," Dante told her with a quick smile.

She watched him carefully. She hadn't seen him in a couple of days. With everything going on, she'd been running from place to place. Last night she'd thought they would get together, but he'd still been at the office when she'd gotten home from the pet store. He'd said he would be working late and not to wait up for him.

She told herself not to read too much into his ac-

tions, but she couldn't shake the feeling that something was wrong. Although if she was asked to say what, she wasn't sure she could.

They stacked the pet care brochures and made sure there were supplies for the animals, along with snacks and items for cleanup. Then Dante pulled out a chair and patted it.

"Have a seat," he told her. "You're going to be on your feet all afternoon."

She sank down and smiled at him. "You sure I can't talk you into staying for the adoption?"

"No, thanks. I'm going back to work. Contracts don't know a holiday season." He grabbed another chair and sat across from her. "When's the first big rehearsal?"

"In three days. I'm excited and nervous. We'll go through the show several times, then have our big dress rehearsal in a week. Then the performance. Ack!"

"You'll get through it."

"I know. I'm telling myself to stay calm. Oh, if you get a chance, you should come to the dress rehearsal. It won't be as crowded as the actual performance."

A muscle in Dante's cheek twitched. "Evie, you remember what we talked about before?"

The question was simple enough, and on the face of it, not very threatening. Even so, her stomach clenched and her throat went dry.

"You'll have to be a little more specific," she said, forcing herself to smile.

"When this started." He motioned to the space between them.

The "this" being their relationship, she thought. "Of course."

"We agreed it would be easy and there wouldn't be any pressure. No expectations."

He was leading up to something, and she just wanted him to get to the point. Because whatever he had to say, it couldn't be good. This was not a lead-in to "I love you and want to spend the rest of my life with you."

She tilted her head and stared at him. "You're stalling, which isn't your style. Get to the point."

"I'm heading out of town in a couple of days. Flying to Aspen. I won't be here for Christmas."

He was leaving? As in leaving? "Oh," she said slowly, thinking maybe the news wasn't all bad. The holidays could be intense. Fool's Gold required a lot of participation, and Dante was still resisting belonging. "I'm sorry you'll miss the show."

"Me, too." He glanced away, then back at her. "An old girlfriend called. She's meeting me there. I'll be back after New Year's."

Evie was pretty sure Dante kept talking, but she couldn't hear any words. There was only a rushing sound and the sensation of her heart being torn apart. She hoped she didn't go pale or pass out.

Instincts for self-preservation kicked in, and in that moment, all she wanted was Dante gone before he could begin to guess how much this was hurting her.

She managed to stand and felt her thighs start to tremble. She moved behind the chair and placed her hand on the back to keep herself upright.

"That's exciting," she said, hoping her voice sounded normal. "Aspen. I've never been. Of course I don't ski or snowboard, so I don't think I've missed that much. You have a good time, though."

Dante studied her. "Evie," he began.

She waved her hand to cut him off. "Don't," she told him. "This is what we agreed to. Just fun, right? Getting each other through the holidays. Mission accomplished. You're going to miss some delicious cookies, but maybe my mom will freeze some for you."

She glanced at her wrist—not that she was wearing a watch. "Oh, look at the time. I need to grab some lunch before the pets arrive. I'll see you after the first of the year."

She released the chair and willed her body to stay strong. All she had to do was grab her bag, and then she could escape. If she could just have a few minutes by herself, she could get her feelings under control and survive the day.

"Evie, wait."

She kept on walking. She could see her purse on a table. She reached for the handle and continued toward the exit. Once outside, she broke into a run. Her previously injured leg protested a little, but not enough to slow her down. She turned at the first corner she came to, and then another, ending up on the edge of the big park in town. It was cold and gray, but there still wasn't any snow.

She put her hand on the bark of a bare tree and tried to catch her breath. Only instead of inhaling, she began to sob. Deep, soul-ripping sobs that welled up from deep inside of her.

He was leaving. Dante was leaving. Worse, he was going to be with someone else. There was another woman he would laugh with and talk to and make love with. Someone else would hear his silly jokes and know the warmth of his body first thing in the morning. Someone else would be with him for Christmas.

After not being willing to trust herself enough to love anyone, she'd finally given her heart, only to have it tossed back at her. Dante didn't love her, and he certainly didn't want her to love him. He'd told her that from the beginning. She just hadn't been listening. She hadn't believed.

And now he was gone, and somehow, she had to get through days and days of activities, including the performance on Christmas Eve.

She gulped in air, then straightened. She could

do it, she told herself. She was strong. She'd handled worse and survived, she would get through this. The trick was to not let anyone know. Sympathy, while well meant, would only make it harder to go on. When Christmas was over, she would figure out how she was supposed to stop loving him, but for now, she would simply put one foot in front of the other. After all, she was used to dancing through the pain.

Eighteen

"I LOVE HIM!"

The girl speaking was maybe six or seven. She hung on to the large black Labrador mix with both arms. The dog, probably four or five and still skinny from being abandoned and trying to survive in the mountains, wagged his tail back and forth, obviously pleased by the turn of events.

Evie did her best to get lost in the moment, to feel happy for the family and their new pet. The young couple took the offered food and the information on care.

"We went to the shelter several times," the wife said happily. "He's perfect for us. We're calling him Wally."

The little girl beamed up at her parents. "I'm so happy, I almost don't need presents this year."

"That's pretty happy," her dad said.

She nodded. "We could ask Santa to take them to children who don't have a new puppy."

The parents exchanged a look of pride and love.

"That's very nice," her mother said. "Let's talk about that when we get home."

Evie handed over their dog license and the rest of the paperwork. "Have a great holiday," she said and watched them walk away, Wally trotting at their side.

"Another happy ending," May said as she walked over with more completed forms in her hand. "We've found homes for all the puppies and kittens, which isn't a surprise but is still nice. Most of the cats are claimed. Someone took all the fish earlier. Did you see that? I don't understand fish as pets. They can't even interact."

"I think you're just supposed to watch them."

"I'd rather watch a movie." Her mother gave her a quick hug. "I see you're adopting that cat."

"Alexander. I'm taking him home with me this afternoon."

"I hope you'll be very happy together." Her mother studied her for a second. "Are you all right? You've been quiet today."

"I'm fine," Evie said quickly. "Just tired from everything I have to get done. The performance isn't that many days away and we start full rehearsals on the actual stage next week. I need to make sure my dancers are comfortable with the entire show. All those seats are intimidating."

She hoped talking about the upcoming performance was enough of a distraction to get her
mother to stop asking questions. Eventually she
would have to come clean about what had happened with Dante, but right now she couldn't talk
about it. Not only was her heart breaking, but she
was also left feeling stupid. It was as if she'd had
a party and no one came. There were decorations
and food and music, but no guests. While she'd
been busy falling in love, Dante had been looking
for a way out. He'd found a good one, too.

All she had to do was get through the rest of
the afternoon. Then she could go home and have
a private meltdown.

May stared at her. Her gaze was so intent that
Evie was sure she'd figured out the truth.

"I know what it is," her mother said at last, then
startled Evie by suddenly starting to cry. "It's all
my fault."

"That's not possible," Evie said, as tears filled
May's eyes and spilled down her cheeks.

"Of course it is. You're my daughter and I love
you so much. But I lost you because I was stupid,
and what if you never forgive me? What if I've
done too much damage? What if you can't forgive me?"

She covered her face with her hands and continued to cry.

Evie stood immobilized by shock. She recognized she was at a crossroads, and whatever she decided at this moment would influence the rest of her life.

Yes, her mother had made mistakes. There were reasons, some better than others, for what had happened, but in the end it came down to a choice. Hang on to the past and stay stuck or forgive and move on.

Which meant no choice at all. There was only what was right. While she was still battered and bruised from what Dante had done, she felt a deeper wound finally heal. It wasn't much right now, but later that healing would give her strength. She wanted and needed to be a part of her family.

She reached for her mother and pulled her close. "You didn't lose me, Mom. I'm right here, and I love you, too."

May looked at her. "You do? You swear?"

"I swear. We still have a long way to go. But I've decided to stay in Fool's Gold. We'll hang out together. You can help me find a place to buy. How's that?"

May hugged her so tight, Evie couldn't breathe. But that was okay. Because right now, this was exactly what she needed.

"I do love you," May told her.

"I know. Now you have to promise to stop apol-

ogizing. The past is done. From now on, we're just going to deal with the present. Together."

May squeezed again. "Thank you. Thank you so much."

Evie shook her head. "I have to thank you, too, Mom. For making the effort. I'm not sure I would have been able to put pride aside and risk reaching out."

"You mean it about staying here?"

"Yes. Dominique wants to expand the dance school, and I have some ideas for that."

"You could do a dance exercise class for women my age. To help us get in shape. Everyone I know wants to move like you do. You're always so graceful."

"I'd like that."

"I'm not sure what we'd call it. Exercise and dance for old women probably isn't a good name."

Evie started to laugh, and her mom joined in.

May sniffed, then glanced around. While no one was overtly watching, Evie was pretty sure they were the center of attention.

"All right then," her mother said, wiping her cheeks. "Is my mascara running?"

"You look beautiful."

May smiled. "I think that's an exaggeration. I'm going to duck into the bathroom and spruce myself up. Then I'll be back and we can see what we can do about getting the rest of these pets adopted."

"HERE IT IS," Evie said, carefully lifting the cat carrier out of the backseat of her car. "I'm sorry to make you ride back here, but I didn't want to have to worry about the air bag deploying. Not that I'm a bad driver and we're at risk for being in an accident."

She pressed her lips together. "I'm babbling, I know. I'm a little nervous. I've already been rejected by one guy in my life. I guess I'm afraid you'll be critical."

She closed the car door and walked into her place.

The previous night she'd set up the cat supplies. She'd put the litter box upstairs in the guest bathroom. She'd folded an old, soft blanket on the window seat in the guest room. On sunny days Alexander could sun himself there.

The food and water bowls were full and on a placemat in a quiet part of her kitchen. She wasn't sure where to put his cat bed. From what she'd read, he would find where he was most comfortable, so for now, it was in a corner, tucked next to a chair. He could see out, but still feel a little protected.

She took the carrier upstairs to the guest room. She figured they would start near the bathroom and let him find his way from there. She set it on the floor and opened the wire door.

"You're home," she said in a quiet voice. "Al-

exander, come on, big guy. This is it. Where you belong."

He slowly, cautiously, stepped out of the carrier. After glancing at her, he walked into the bathroom and sniffed. He paused at the litter box, but didn't use it.

"I hope I got the right kind," she said. "It has baking soda in it."

He walked past her and went under the guest bed. Before she could wonder if he was going to hide there for a while, he came out the other side and headed for the hallway.

She'd closed the door to the master, thinking she didn't want to confuse him. He headed downstairs, and she followed.

He made a circuit of the rest of the place, pausing to delicately lap at the water and sniff the dry food. Then he walked to the sofa, jumped up and stared at her.

She paused at the bottom of the stairs.

"I should probably tell you about myself," she murmured, thinking she was being an idiot, but not sure how else to start a conversation with a cat.

"I've never had a pet before, so it's possible I won't get everything right. If you could just be a little patient with me, I would appreciate it. I'm, um, a dance teacher, which I like a lot. Do you like children? Because there might be some around,

from time to time. I just broke up with the guy I was seeing."

Evie paused, feeling the pain of the words. "I thought he was pretty great. I thought..." She swallowed against the tightness in her throat. "I was in love with him," she whispered, fighting tears. "Stupid, huh?"

She crossed to the sofa, sitting at the opposite end from Alexander, so as not to frighten him. "I've never had a successful romantic relationship, so it's really just going to be the two of us. But I'm hoping you and I can get along. I want to take good care of you."

Steady green eyes regarded her.

"It would really help if you could tell me what you're thinking," she said.

Alexander stood and walked across the back of the sofa. He jumped down on the cushion next to her and then sat, looking at her. Slowly, carefully, she reached out to pet him. She stroked the length of his back, then rubbed the side of his face. When she scratched under his chin, he raised his head up and forward.

"Do you like that?" she asked. "Is that nice?"

Without warning, he jumped onto her lap and stood facing her. She rubbed his soft fur. He turned once and then curled up on her lap and began to purr.

She continued to pet him, feeling the quiet rum-

ble as she rubbed his chin. More tears fell. She didn't try to stop them. She knew that acknowledging the pain was a part of the process. Eventually she would heal, and one day she would be able to look back, saying she'd learned something. Until then she had to figure out a way to survive with a Dante-size hole in her heart.

EVIE FOUGHT AGAINST a pounding headache. She'd spent most of Sunday holed up in her townhouse, getting to know her new cat and sobbing uncontrollably. She'd been forced to duck out for food in the afternoon, then had retreated to her ongoing pity party.

For a second night, she'd mostly been awake, staring at the ceiling, wondering what she could have done differently and asking impossible questions. Like was she ever going to meet "the one" and fall in love?

Alexander had settled the issue of his sleeping arrangements by joining her. He was a thoughtful roommate, curling up at the foot of the bed and sleeping silently. When she'd started crying again at four in the morning, he'd draped himself across her chest and had purred until she'd managed to calm herself.

This morning she'd heard Dante leave around five. As it was way too early for work, she'd assumed he'd been leaving for the airport. Sure

enough, she'd checked the parking lot by his office and his car wasn't there. He was well and truly
gone, flying off to be with another woman.

All of which made her heart break more but
wasn't anything she could deal with right now.
After spending the past two hours working with
the lighting guy, she had to pull herself together
for the dance rehearsal. This would be the first full
run-through, with music and lights. Based on her
professional experience, it could go very badly and
it was up to her to stay calm and positive.

Every part of her hurt. Her eyes were puffy,
and she was pale. Falling in love was a bitch, she
told herself, but no one else's problem. She had to
pull it together for her girls and for the town. In
less than a week, she would be done with all this
and able to freak out as much as she wanted. She
planned to spend the day after Christmas having
an emotional meltdown. That would be the end of
it. On the twenty-seventh, she would get her act
together and move on with her life. What was that
saying? She would fake it until she made it.

The rehearsal was due to start at two. By one
forty-five all her dancers were there. Grace, the
lithe, talented star of the school, had gathered the
girls who had the most trouble with their steps and
taken them through their section. The tap team
was going through their routine, their stocking feet

silent on the stage. The rest of the groups were practicing, as well.

Short and tall, skinny and round. All working hard. Happy and determined, she thought.

Gideon walked up to the stage. "Hey," he said. "I'm here to be the voice from beyond."

She turned to him. "Aren't they amazing?" she asked.

He glanced at the girls and nodded. "Beautiful and unique."

"So speaks the Zen master."

"Have you been practicing your breathing?"

"Sure. In my free time. I'm also working on a plan for peace in the Middle East."

"Let me know how that goes."

She waited until he'd climbed the steps up to the stage, then followed him back behind the side curtains. He would watch the show and do the narration from there. For the dress rehearsal and the actual show, he would be farther away from the action, so there wasn't background noise. At that point, they would depend on musical cues to stay in sync.

"Thanks for doing this," she said as she handed him the microphone. "I know it's been a lot of time."

He shrugged. "I got the music together and learned a script. No big deal."

Her voice got a little tight. "It is to me. And the girls. Plus, you're here. We can depend on you."

Gideon's dark eyes narrowed. "Uh-oh. What does that mean?"

"Nothing. Sorry. Personal stuff."

He took a step back. "Are you okay?"

"No, but let's not talk about it."

"What happened?"

She drew in a breath. She was going to have to start telling people at some point. She could practice now. Get the first telling over with. After all, Gideon wasn't a close friend or part of her family.

"Dante and I broke up. I guess it's more accurate to say we're not seeing each other anymore. Breaking up implies a relationship. We never had that." She felt her eyes starting to burn and blinked away the tears. "It's fine. Or it will be. I just wish I hadn't fallen in love with him, you know."

Gideon's face took on the expression of a trapped animal. Despite the ache in her heart, she started to laugh.

"I'll stop talking now," she said. "You look like you're going to faint."

"I don't like the emotional stuff."

"But you're all one with the universe."

"That's different. I can be in the moment."

"As long as it's not an emotional moment?"

"So the system is flawed." He seemed to gather strength. "Are you all right? Can I, ah, help?"

"You're sweet, but, no. I'm fine." She grinned. "So the big tough guy thing is just an act?"

"Some people are afraid of spiders."

"You're afraid of emotions."

He shuddered. "I avoid them. But I could storm a South American country and overthrow a dictator if that would help."

"Not this week, but I do appreciate the offer." She stared at him. "You're really strange."

"I get that a lot." He picked up one of the two microphones and handed it to her. "I'm ready whenever you are."

"I'll get the girls."

She walked to the center of the stage. Gideon was dangerous, she thought. The kind of man who knew things, had seen things, the rest of the world could only guess at. But in the end, Dante was more lethal. Gideon might be capable of overthrowing a government, but Dante had shattered her heart.

The really sad part was if he walked in the door this second and begged her to take him back, she would. In a second. Which meant a trip to the self-help section of the local bookstore was in order. She needed some serious healing.

But that, too, was for later.

She turned on the microphone and faced her dancers.

"Thank you all for coming," she said. "I'm so

excited about this show. Each of you has worked so hard. You should be proud of yourselves." She paused and smiled. "All right. Let's start from the top, shall we?"

Nineteen

"HEY, BIG GUY," Evie said as she walked into her townhouse. She'd just taken her dancers through a second day of rehearsing the entire show. "It went really well. I'm so proud of them."

She paused in the living room, not sure where to find Alexander. The cat had only been living with her for a few days, and they didn't have much of a routine yet. But as she shrugged out of her coat, she heard a soft "meow" from the stairs.

Alexander stood about halfway down, his green eyes wide, his expression expectant.

"Hi, you," she said, walking toward him. "How was your afternoon? Did you sleep in the sun?"

She moved up a few steps, and he moved down. They met somewhere near the bottom. She sank onto the carpeted stairs and began to stroke him. He stepped close and rubbed his head against her hand. His kitty eyes closed, and he purred.

"Wow, that's some greeting," she said. She

slowly picked him up, careful to support his rear, and held him in her arms. He relaxed against her, his whole body vibrating with a contented rumble.

"I'm going to assume you're happy to see me and not anticipating that dinner is in a few minutes."

She set him on her lap. He planted his back feet on her thighs and put his front paw on her chest, by her collarbones, then pressed his nose to hers.

She laughed and scratched his chin. "Okay, so that act in the shelter was you playing hard to get, right? You were making sure I was committed before you gave your kitty heart. I can respect that." Her smile faded. "I should have done the same with Dante. Then I wouldn't feel so sucky about the whole falling in love thing."

She scooped him up in her arms and carried him down the stairs. "I stopped at the pet store and got you some canned food to try." She set him down and reached for the small paper bag she'd carried in with her. "It's organic and supposed to be very supportive of your urinary health. Apparently we're going to have to watch that."

Alexander followed her into the kitchen. She served him a couple of teaspoons of the canned food on a dish and watched him polish off the snack. When he'd finished, he glanced up at her.

"Nice?" she asked. "That was the chicken flavor. I also got tuna."

She put a lid on the can and stuck it in the refrigerator, then paused to survey the complete lack of people food. While she'd gone to the store, her efforts had been halfhearted at best. She had eggs and milk, along with a couple of apples. In the freezer were a few frozen entrées.

She could order a pizza, she thought. Or go get takeout. But that would be so much effort. It had been different with Dante. Easier. She missed that, and his energy. She missed how he made her laugh and the way she felt in his arms. Mostly she missed him.

Before she could make a decision, or simply collapse on the floor and give in to tears, she heard a knock on the door. For a second, her heart froze.

"It's not Dante," she whispered. "He's gone. Off having sex with an old girlfriend."

She walked to the living room and pulled open the door. Instead of a lost tourist or a kid selling who-knows-what, she found herself staring at Patience, Heidi, Annabelle, Charlie and several other women it took her a second to place. She saw her mother waving from the back of the group.

"Hi," she said, not sure what was going on. All the women were holding grocery bags. Was this a shopping intervention?

"We heard," Heidi said. "About what happened."

"This is not the time to be delicate," Charlie said. "We know Dante is a complete jackass and

we're sorry." She held up a bottle of vodka in one hand and Baileys mint chocolate liqueur in the other. "We're here to help."

Evie stepped back, mostly because her porch was small and she couldn't figure out how to tell them all to go away.

"I'm Pia," a pretty brunette said. "We've met, but you probably don't remember."

"I brought my own blender," Jo, from Jo's Bar, told her, holding up a very professional-looking machine. "And ice. I didn't know if you had an icemaker."

"Oh, honey," her mother said and pulled her close. "I'm so sorry about Dante."

The women trooped into her living room which, fortunately, was clean. One of the triplets came out holding Alexander.

"I'm Dakota and he's adorable."

"Thanks. I just adopted him last Saturday."

Dakota nodded. "Thanks for the heads-up. I'll warn everyone."

Still confused, Evie followed her into the living room.

"We have a new-to-the-family cat here, ladies," Dakota said, patting Alexander. "Let's try to keep it down."

Evie still wasn't sure what "it" was, although it obviously involved total strangers taking over her house. Jo had already set up her blender and

was pouring generous amounts of liquor in with ice. Someone had set out martini glasses and little candy canes.

Charlie was putting out bowls of what looked like dip and guacamole. There were regular chips, tortilla chips, crackers and spreads, plates of cookies, brownies and the largest box of fudge she'd ever seen.

"I'm doing a nonalcoholic cranberry sparkler as soon as I get these peppermint martinis done," Jo called. "For Annabelle and Nevada."

"For me, too," Heidi said. "I ate way too much last night and my tummy's been unhappy all day."

Evie met her sister-in-law's gaze but didn't say a word. Heidi's problem had nothing to do with the volume of food she'd eaten and everything to do with being pregnant. But Evie was going to keep her secret.

Charlie walked up to her and put her arm around her shoulders. "Gideon came to me this morning," she said. "I made a few calls and here we are. We would have come sooner, but you had your rehearsal and we didn't want to get in the way."

"I don't understand," Evie told her.

"It's a Fool's Gold thing. We come, we show support, we get drunk and eat crap. You cry."

"In front of everyone?"

"Trust me, you'll feel better."

"Did you go through this?"

"No. I ran because I wasn't brave enough to face my friends. But you're tougher than me."

"How can you say that?" Charlie was the most impressive person Evie knew.

Charlie stared at her. "Evie, look at yourself. You've been on your own since you were seventeen, with no support. You practically raised yourself and you turned out great. Two months into a new job, you get the whole *Dance of the Winter King* dumped on you and you manage to pull it all together. Who else could do that?"

It was a question she didn't know how to answer. Honestly, she'd never thought of herself as special. In her mind, she'd actually screwed up a lot. She wasn't talented enough to stay in Juilliard and she'd never been able to settle on a job she loved. Until now.

"I'm sorry about Dante," Charlie told her. "For what it's worth, I think he's going to regret losing you for the rest of his life."

"I really hope so."

Charlie grinned. "That's my girl."

Evie was led into the living room and settled in the middle of the sofa. All the other women gathered around. Her mom sat next to her. Jo handed out the peppermint martinis, which turned out to be delicious and went down far too easily.

Evie sipped, aware that everyone was watching her.

"I'll start," a redhead said. She was sitting cross-legged on the floor, Alexander draped over one thigh. "I'm Liz, by the way. Married to Ethan." She pointed at the triplets. "He's their brother."

Nevada groaned. "I suppose that makes what he did our fault?"

Liz laughed. "Technically, it does."

"We're sorry," Montana told her.

"I accept your apology." Liz turned back to Evie. "Ethan and I had a past, which made things complicated."

"And a kid," Charlie said.

"Yes. A son that Ethan didn't know about. When things got ugly, I didn't know what to do. I was trapped here, alone. But everyone came through for me."

"Me, too," Heidi said. "When Rafe was being stupid, my friends had buttons printed up. Team Heidi and Team Rafe." She smiled smugly. "There were a lot more Team Heidi buttons around town."

Charlie shrugged. "I can't bond. I ran."

While Evie appreciated the stories, they all had something in common. Each of the men in question might have acted stupid, but in the end, one by one, they'd come around. There was a shiny wedding band on every left-hand ring finger. Well, except for Annabelle and Charlie, who had engagement rings. No one in this room had lost the man of her dreams. Only Evie.

She swallowed against the familiar tightness in her throat. The last thing she wanted was to start crying. The problem was, she knew the truth. There wouldn't be a happy ending for her. Not really. Dante had the best reason of all to avoid love. He believed the emotion was dangerous. His mother had died because he'd fallen in love.

Tears filled her eyes. She fought them, but one trickled onto her cheek, followed by another. Her mother pulled her close.

"Remind yourself he's a jerk, and one day you won't be in love with him anymore," May murmured.

"Does saying that help?"

"No, but eventually it turns out to be true. You go ahead and cry. When you're done, we'll have ice cream, and I happen to know that really does help."

EVIE'S BREAKUP PARTY HANGOVER lasted for nearly two days. The first day she'd had to excuse herself twice from rehearsal to go throw up, and if she never, ever tasted peppermint again in her life, it would be too soon. The second day the only lingering effects of the alcohol and cookies was a gently pounding headache. On the morning of the third day, she woke feeling like her regular self.

She rolled over and found Alexander was already up and busy with his morning ablutions. She watched him carefully wash his face, first licking

the side of his paw, then wiping it across his face
and over his ear. He was thorough and patient, but
in the end, clean.

"'Morning," she said when he looked up at her.

He started to purr and walked toward her for his
cuddle. She pulled him next to her and rubbed him
all over before finishing with a good chin scratch.

"You've been very good to me," she told him.
"I was really stupid with the martinis. That won't
happen again. I've learned my lesson. About liquor if not love."

She rolled onto her back and stared at the ceiling. She'd never been in love before, so had no
idea how long it took to feel better. One thing she
knew for sure. As soon as she got through the
holidays, she was going to start looking for a new
place. There was no way she could live next door
to Dante. She would be around him too much to
forget him.

Her friends would help with finding a place, she
thought, that knowledge easing some of the pain.
Plus her mom had offered to loan her the money
for a down payment. Knowing May, she would
probably want to make it a gift, but Evie would
prefer to pay her back. It seemed the grown-up
thing to do.

"Would you like a yard?" she asked. "Do you
like going outside? I can see you lying in the grass,
sunning."

Alexander draped across her, his eyes half-closed, his purr comforting her.

She would keep busy, she told herself. Maybe take some classes at the college. There were also her ideas for the expanded teaching schedule. And that exercise class her mom had mentioned sounded fun.

"I'm going to get over him," she told her cat. "I swear I will."

But the ache in her heart seemed bigger every day, and sometimes she wondered how anyone survived losing a great love. How did you learn to forget? To be happy again? She wondered if maybe that was simply a matter of finding small joys in life and stringing them together. Maybe after a while they became bigger than the pain.

She could only hope.

"OKAY," GIDEON SAID from his place backstage. "They win."

Evie looked at the nearly sixty excited, squealing, running, jumping and dancing girls careening around the stage and nodded. "Right there with you. I feel like if we back away slowly and don't show fear, they won't attack."

It was the long-anticipated afternoon of the dress rehearsal. Everyone was in costume for a run-through of the show. Wings quivered, sequins glittered and tap shoes rang out on the wooden

stage. Evie had been worried about getting the girls dressed and having them work with their costumes. What she hadn't anticipated was the excitement that would send them into a giggling, bouncing frenzy.

She told herself to simply pick up the microphone and speak with authority. That the girls would instantly quiet and listen. What she didn't know was what she was going to do if she was wrong.

"Breathing isn't helping," Gideon said quietly. "I don't like that."

"They're my responsibility," Evie told him. "I'm going in."

But before she could gather her courage, the door to the convention center opened and Dominique swept inside, followed by Morgan, who played the Winter King.

The petite former dancer moved with a grace that captivated the girls. As one, they turned to watch the elegantly dressed woman. Dominique's hair was perfectly coiffed. She had on a trim, tailored suit, the color of her green eyes, and four-inch heels. She stopped in front of the stage and faced the students.

"Good afternoon, ladies."

"Good afternoon, Ms. Guérin," they answered in unison.

Dominique offered a smile. "I see you're all

ready for your dress rehearsal. What I want you to remember as you prepare for your moment in the spotlight is that each of you is a star. A beautiful shining light that will transform those privileged enough to see you."

She paused. "When I danced professionally there were times when I was tired or hurt or ill. Times when I didn't want to gather myself enough to give my all, but I always did. I remembered that, while this was just one performance for me, this was a memory for everyone watching. They had taken time out of their lives to come see me. They wanted to experience the joy and beauty that only comes from dance. They wanted the experience."

Evie glanced around. Every single girl was staring, riveted by the famous woman's words.

"You will give them that experience. Each of you will offer a memory that can be carried a lifetime. When you feel nervous, breathe deeply. If you start to shake, focus on the music. Evie has taught you well. We are both so proud of you, and I am very much looking forward to watching each of you perform."

Talk about a memory, Evie thought, clapping for her boss, as the girls joined in. For the rest of their lives her students would remember being encouraged by Dominique Guérin.

Evie stepped toward the stage. "Thank you,

Dominique. Now, let's all move offstage. Gideon will start the music and we'll take it from the top."

Nervous energy now channeled productively, the dancers did as she asked. Evie turned off the microphone and walked over to her boss.

"Thank you for this. You're exactly what they needed."

"I'm very excited about the show." Dominique put her hand on Evie's arm. "I heard about your young man. I'm so sorry. After Christmas I'm visiting with friends in Fiji for a few weeks. If you feel the need to get away, I'm happy to loan you my apartment in New York. Charlie has the key."

The unexpected generosity had Evie's eyes feeling a little moist. "Thank you. That's very sweet."

"Some men are idiots."

"I keep telling myself that. So far it's not working, but soon, I hope."

The opening bars of the first song filled the convention center. Morgan settled into his throne as Gideon's smooth chocolate-and-velvet voice spoke over the music.

"Once upon a time there was a magical kingdom ruled by a kind and generous king. He was blessed with many daughters. Each beautiful and wise. The king loved his daughters so much, he decided he would keep them with him forever."

The first group danced onto the stage, their wings quivering and catching the light.

Evie turned her attention to them. Whatever happened or didn't happen with Dante was out of her control. Good ending or bad, she would get through it. Not because she was especially tough or determined, but because she wasn't alone. She had her friends and her family. People who loved her. She belonged, and right now that was more than enough.

ON THE DAY BEFORE the performance, Evie knew the show was going to be brilliant. Beyond brilliant. Her dancers were amazing, taking to the stage with grace and style. Their costumes fit perfectly, the music was fabulous and Gideon's changes to the narration added a heartwarming element that would have everyone in tears.

She walked into the convention center a half hour before rehearsal, knowing that between them, she and her girls had reason to be proud of themselves. There were—

Her cell phone rang.

Evie grabbed it and glanced at the unfamiliar but local number. "Hello?"

"Evie? Is that you?"

"Yes. Who is this?" She didn't recognize the woman's voice, but she sounded very upset.

"It's Shelley, Grace's mom. I'm so sorry, but there's been an accident." Shelley took a breath. "Grace and her friends went up the mountain this

morning to find snow. Unfortunately, they also went snowboarding. I'd warned her not to, what with the show tomorrow and everything, but she snuck off. She slipped and fell and broke her leg."

Evie sank onto the nearest chair. "Is she all right?"

"Yes. It's a clean break. They barely had to do anything to set it, but she won't be dancing anytime soon. She's hysterical, of course. I was terrified, but now that I know she's okay, I'm hoping this teaches her to be more responsible. Teenagers. Which doesn't help you at all. Like I said, I'm so sorry."

"Don't worry about the dance," Evie said automatically, relieved Grace was going to be fine. "We'll figure something out."

"We'll all be there tomorrow night, to watch. Grace will be in tears, just so you're braced."

"Of course she's disappointed."

"And then some. Okay, I need to run. I have to get Grace home. See you tomorrow."

"Bye."

Evie disconnected the call, then stared at the phone, not sure what she was supposed to do. Grace had a full minute solo in the most critical part of the story. It was her dance that finally convinced her father to let the girls go into the world. Her dance began the transformation.

Evie dug through her bag and stared at the

notes she'd made. There was no way to change the music, so there had to be a one-minute transition. Something simple, she thought, wondering who could learn a new dance in a day. She was still working on options when her students began to arrive.

She waited until they were all there to tell them what had happened.

Abby Sutton rolled her eyes when she heard. "It's because she likes this boy who loves to snowboard."

Melissa nudged her sister. "Shh. Don't say that."

"Why not? It's true. Girls do stupid things for boys."

Talk about telling the truth, Evie thought. She'd been an idiot over a guy herself.

"While I'm sure we all feel badly for Grace," Evie said instead, "we have to come up with a way to fill the beats in the music. Grace had a solo at a pivotal moment in the story."

Lillie shrugged. "Why don't you do it?"

Evie blinked at her. "Me? I can't."

"Why not? You know all the steps. You know everyone's steps." Lillie giggled. "You could do the whole show yourself."

"That would look pretty silly," Evie told her.

Melissa and Abby glanced at each other, then back at her.

"You should do it," Abby told her.

"Yeah," Melissa said. "You're better than all of us. Even Grace."

Several girls nodded at that. Then they were all telling Evie to dance the solo.

"You can be one of the daughters, just like us," Lillie said. "Please say you will."

"I'd have to check with Ms. Guérin," Evie said, not wanting to take the spotlight from her students.

"She'll think it's fun," Abby said confidently. "Besides, if you dance in the show, you get to wear makeup and have your hair done. And that's the best part."

Twenty

DANTE STOOD AT the window of his suite, looking out at the mountains. The room was large and well furnished, the view amazing. Logs crackled in the fireplace. New snow beckoned, and room service had just delivered breakfast. Everything was perfect, and he should be one happy guy. Only he wasn't. He'd been through some crappy holidays since his mother's death, but he had to admit this was the worst.

He wasn't anywhere he wanted to be, and he sure as hell wasn't with anyone who interested him. He was alone, on a mountain, on Christmas Eve, and for the life of him he couldn't figure out why he'd thought this was a good idea.

When he'd realized he'd gone too far with Evie, leaving had seemed like the only option. It would make the break quick and clean. He'd thought that would be easiest for her. He'd made up a story about a former girlfriend so Evie wouldn't think

they'd get back together when he returned. Then he'd taken off. He'd assumed that by the time the plane landed in Colorado, he would have forgotten all about her.

Only he hadn't. He thought about her constantly. There were plenty of single women at the resort, and more than one of them had made it clear she was interested. He couldn't have been less so. He didn't want just some woman—he wanted Evie. He missed her. He missed talking to her at the end of the day and thinking about her when he should be working. He missed their dinners, their nights, their mornings. He missed everything about her.

Worse, he missed Fool's Gold. He missed the stupid decorations and the idiotic people greeting him every other second when he walked down the street. He missed his friends, and he missed Evie more than he'd thought possible.

Right now she was getting ready for the Live Nativity, which this year would feature an elephant. Where else but Fool's Gold? And was he there, secretly having the time of his life? No. He was stuck in some damn suite in Aspen.

He stalked across the room and told himself he had to get over this. Over her. He had to figure out a way to stop caring about her. Because if he didn't, he would be in real danger. He would start imagining being with her for a long time. Months even. He would start to imagine that it was okay

for him to have feelings and then he would… He
would…

Dante stopped in the middle of the room. He
turned in a slow circle, as if not sure where he
was or what to do next. He needed to get home,
he realized. Not just to Fool's Gold, but to Evie.
Because… Well, hell, he was just going to say it.

"I love her."

That's what his heart had been trying to tell
him. He needed her and wanted to be with her. He
wanted to give her everything he had and know
that she felt the same. He wanted to hold her and
protect her and maybe even, someday, have children with her.

He'd only risked his heart once before, and that
had cost him everything. So he'd vowed never to
take that chance again. But this time he couldn't
help himself. Sometime when he hadn't been paying attention, Evie had stolen his heart. The killer
was, he didn't want it back. She could have it. If
she wanted it.

He ran to the phone and punched in the number
for the concierge.

"This is Dante Jefferson, in suite 587. I need to
book a flight out of here today."

There was a moment of silence. "Um, sir, you
do realize it's Christmas Eve? There aren't going
to be any flights. It's going to take a miracle for
you to find a seat."

"I'm thinking that maybe miracles do happen, so let's give it a try." He grinned. "Actually don't bother looking for a commercial flight. Find me a private plane. Money is no object."

"All right. Where are you flying to?"

"Fool's Gold, California."

"MOMMY, WHY DOES Baby Jesus have an elephant?"

Evie smiled at the question. The little boy stared up at Priscilla, his expression one of awe.

"Baby Jesus loves all the animals," the boy's mom said.

"Can I have an elephant?"

"Not this year."

"Can I have a puppy?"

"We'll talk about it with your dad."

May linked her arm with Evie's and sighed. "I do love a good nativity."

"This one is very special."

It was midday on Christmas Eve, and the Live Nativity had drawn a huge crowd. Most of the animals had come from the Castle Ranch. The sheep, a couple of goats, Reno the pony and Wilbur the pig. Along with Priscilla, of course.

There were people playing the main roles, although a doll stood in for Baby Jesus. There had been talk of a live infant, but when the temperatures had dropped below freezing, the substitution had been made.

"Are you nervous?" May asked in a whisper.

Evie touched her stomach where butterflies had taken up residence.

"More than I would have thought possible," she admitted. "I haven't danced on a stage in a long time."

"You'll be wonderful. I can't wait to see you. We're getting there early so we can sit up front."

"I'm not sure if that's news that's going to make me feel better," Evie admitted.

Dominique had been thrilled with the idea of her taking over Grace's solo. Evie had spent much of the previous evening practicing. Gideon had come by to cue the music and had stayed through her session.

He was a good guy. Unfortunately she couldn't summon the least little tingle when he was around. And based on how he'd treated her pretty much as a sister, she would say the same was true for him. She was going to have to get over Dante the old-fashioned way. With time and ice cream.

But that was for after Christmas. She'd decided that for the holiday itself, she was going to simply go with her feelings. She was going to love him and not fight it. On the twenty-sixth, she would give herself a stern talking-to and load her freezer with Ben & Jerry's.

"I need to get home," Evie said, kissing her mother's cheek. "I have a thousand details to worry

about. Nothing to actually do, but plenty to sweat over."

"We'll see you tonight." May smiled at her. "Should I say break a leg?"

"After what happened to Grace, probably not."

Evie left. She walked back to her house. She saw Alexander sitting in the upstairs window seat. When he saw her, he stood and stretched, then jumped down. She knew he would be waiting on the stairs when she unlocked the door.

She cut across the lawn, then came to a stop as the first snowflakes of the season silently drifted down from the sky.

Evie glanced up at the gray sky, then back at the snow dotting the shoulders and sleeves of her jacket. Then she spun in a circle and started to laugh.

"IT'S STILL SNOWING," Lillie said, plopping down next to Evie.

Evie glanced at the girl and smiled. "You look adorable."

Lillie grinned. "I love my wings."

"You look good in wings."

"Maybe I should have asked Santa for wings instead of a dad."

Evie blinked. "You asked for a dad?"

Lillie wrinkled her nose and leaned close. "I'm old enough to know there's really no Santa, but

it doesn't hurt to ask, right? Only Mom says it doesn't work that way."

She leaned close as Evie finished sewing on her shoes' ribbons.

"You have to do that with every pair of pointe shoes?" Lillie asked.

"Uh-huh." Evie showed her where she'd already softened the toe box.

"You can't just buy them finished?"

"It doesn't work that way. Every dancer wants her shoes the way she likes them."

Evie slipped on the shoes, then tied the ribbons and went up on pointe. She walked a couple of steps, came back down, then sank onto the stage floor.

"It's a lot to do," Lillie said.

"It is." Evie flexed her foot and tied the ribbon in place. After cutting the ends, she used clear nail polish to seal them. "I need to put this stuff away."

"Okay."

They both stood. Evie dropped the nail polish and scissors into her bag. By then the ends were dry. She tucked them under the ribbon around her ankle so it was out of sight. A quick check of the large clock on the wall told her they had ten minutes.

"Okay, everyone," she called. "Let's get in place."

Gideon walked by, his headphones and microphone in place. "We're good," he told her.

Morgan, their king for the evening, settled into his throne and gave her a thumbs-up. The dancers separated into their sections and waited for the musical cue. Dominique stepped onto the stage and began with an explanation of the dance. Seconds later, the music began and the curtain went up.

Evie stood with the other girls and watched the younger girls in wings twirl to the center of the stage. Gideon told the story of the Winter King and his beautiful daughters, and the girls danced.

They had energy and enthusiasm. If there was a bent arm here and a misstep there, Evie didn't notice. She waved girls in place and offered an encouraging whisper when she saw a case of nerves. The music flowed and shifted with each section, and at last it was her turn.

She rose on pointe and made her way across the stage. The dance came easily to her, allowing her to feel the music and get lost in the movements. For a second she allowed herself to miss Dante, to wish things could be different, but then she got out of her head and let her body take over.

Gideon's velvety voice told how the king, so moved by his daughter's beauty and joy, realized he must allow his children to go out into the world. They all returned to the stage and danced together,

spinning until the girls became snowflakes that fell from the ceiling, and the stage went dark.

There was a moment of silence before the audience exploded into delighted applause. Evie stayed where she was, on the floor of the stage, her arms stretched forward. She rose slowly, the signal for the rest of the girls to do the same. As they'd practiced several times, they formed lines and walked forward, then bowed as one. The first group circled around to the back, and the process was repeated several times until all the girls had had a chance to bow and be applauded.

By the end, the audience was on its feet. The girls gathered around Evie for a group hug as they laughed and jumped up and down. Then a dozen or so young boys climbed the stairs and starting handing out small bouquets of flowers to each of the girls. Parents were clapping and trying to capture everything on their camcorders. Mayor Marsha walked out, a massive bouquet of dark red roses in her arms.

She crossed to Evie and handed her the flowers. "I wish I could say these are from the town," she said, speaking into a handheld microphone. "Although we did buy you flowers, they aren't nearly as lovely as these. Perhaps you would like to thank the person responsible personally."

She motioned to the other side of the stage. Evie

turned and nearly collapsed when she saw Dante walking toward her.

He looked tired, she thought, unable to grasp that he was here. Tired and worried, but, oh, so appealing in a cream-colored sweater and jeans. His blue gaze settled on her face as he moved across the stage.

Hope battled with pain and fear. She was thrilled to see him and terrified she would start crying. She wanted to believe his being here was a good thing, but what if there was some busty blonde waiting in the wings?

Dante walked up to her and took both her hands in his. "You were beautiful," he murmured. "You're so talented, and I can't get over what you did with these kids."

"Who's he calling kids?" Evie heard Melissa grumble.

"You're supposed to be in Aspen."

"I was. By myself," he added. "There's no ex-girlfriend."

Relief threatened her ability to stand a second time. "Then why did you say there was?"

"Because I'm an idiot. I thought…" He squeezed her hands. "Evie, I was scared. Scared of what you'd come to mean to me. Scared of my feelings. You know about my mom and what happened. I promised myself I would never let myself care

again. I was doing a good job, too. Until I met you. And then I couldn't help myself."

She was aware of three thousand, two hundred people in the audience, watching. Based on the silence, she would guess that overhead microphones were picking up every word. Not that she was willing to ask Dante to hold that thought so they could go somewhere more private.

"I figured it out this morning. It was Christmas Eve and I wasn't with the people I love. In the place I love. I wasn't with you, Evie. So I chartered a plane to get here in time to see you dance. I knew how much this night meant to you and I wanted to share it with you. I also wanted to tell you that I love you."

Her breath caught. The girls on the stage sighed, as did most of the women watching. Somebody in the audience said something about this "being just like when Shane proposed to Annabelle."

"You do?" she asked.

"Very much. I never believed there could be 'the one' until I met you." He smiled. "I love you and I hope you can forgive me for leaving like that. It will never happen again."

"I believe you."

"About which part?"

"About all of it." The last pain faded away, and her heart began to heal. "I love you, too. I have for a while."

She had more to say, but Dante was pulling her close and kissing her. She wrapped her arms around him and held on. She heard cheers and applause, but they weren't as interesting as the man who held her as if he would never let her go.

SOMETIME LATER, WHEN EVIE had changed her clothes and everyone else had left, she and Dante walked back to their townhouses. It was still snowing, quieting the world and making her feel as if they were all alone...in the best way possible.

"I really am sorry about being such an idiot," Dante told her. "I hurt you. There's no excuse for that."

"I'll let you make it up to me."

"I'd appreciate that."

She glanced at him. "But I do have to tell you that there's a new man in my life."

Dante stared at her. "You went out with Gideon. I knew it."

"No. I got a cat."

He let out a relieved laugh. "Okay. I can handle a cat."

"I don't know. He's pretty handsome and affectionate. And he's a great cuddler."

"You're saying I have my work cut out for me."

"I'm saying we'll have to see who I like better."

He leaned down and wrapped his arms around her waist, then spun them both in a circle. Evie

laughed and held her arms out. Being in love really was like flying.

When her head was spinning, he lowered her to the ground and kissed her. "Merry Christmas, my love," he whispered.

"Merry Christmas."

Still wrapped in each other's arms, they made their way home. Tomorrow was for family and friends, but tonight…tonight was theirs alone.

* * * * *

If you loved A FOOL'S GOLD CHRISTMAS,
turn the page for a special preview of
CHRISTMAS ON 4TH STREET,
available now!

...She...at...go...
She stared around...note...how the nose of
her car was firmly packed in the wall of a surprisingly tall drift. There...d news...she...she...
close to her destination...he bad news was she was
going to have to...but a way to get down the
mountain when...have time to leave.

That was for later, she told herself as she turned
off the engine, then unfastened her seat belt. First
she had a puppy to let out.

One

IN REAL LIFE, snow was not nearly as delightful as it appeared in movies and on TV, Noelle Perkins thought as her spinning car finally came to a stop in a snowbank. She'd been driving up the side of the mountain, not making any sudden moves, when it happened. However, she wasn't exactly sure what the *it* was. There'd been a swoosh and a swerve and then the world twirling around her. There might have been a scream or two, but as she was alone, she wasn't going to admit to that.

She glanced around, noticing how the nose of her car was firmly planted in the wall of a surprisingly firm drift. The good news was she was pretty close to her destination. The bad news was she was going to have to figure out a way to get down the mountain when it was time to leave.

That was for later, she told herself as she turned off the engine, then unfastened her seat belt. First she had a puppy to let out.

Noelle opened the door and started to stand, only to discover why her car had gone whirling around. Snow, it seemed, was slippery. Her feet started to go out from under her and she had to grab the door frame to keep from falling.

"This is so wrong," she murmured, finding her balance and carefully closing the car door. She started walking very tentatively toward the house at the end of the long driveway.

Snow had come early to Fool's Gold. There had been several inches in late October, then it had all gone away. More had fallen in early November and now this blast the following week. But it was different in town, she thought as she felt her left foot slowly sliding out from under her.

She waved her arms and managed to stay on her feet, then started forward again. In town, roads were plowed and sidewalks scraped. Someone put magical stuff down so it wasn't slippery. She never had any trouble in town.

Growing up in Florida, followed by a career move to Los Angeles, had not prepared her for a real winter, she thought as she made it to the porch. Her feet started slipping again. She lunged for the railing and managed to hang on as her lower body slipped and stretched until she was nearly parallel to the ground.

She dug her toes into the snow and ice, hoping to find some traction. At last she managed to

get her legs back under her and straighten. It was like being a cartoon character, she thought grimly. Only with the possibility of breaking bones.

"This is so not what I expected," she said aloud, thinking that Felicia's request had seemed so reasonable. With everyone running around, Webster, her friend's eight-month-old puppy, had been left home alone. Could Noelle go and let him out?

Felicia had been a good friend to Noelle. When Noelle had opened her own store—The Christmas Attic—over Labor Day weekend, Felicia had been right there, helping stock the place and offering suggestions. When Noelle had wanted to participate in town advertising with the other local retailers, Felicia had helped her navigate the maze that was local government regulations. When Noelle worried that she would never find a man for... well, you know, let alone love, Felicia reassured her that it would happen. So helping with the family puppy seemed the least she could do to pay back her friend.

"I am capable," Noelle told herself as she made it up the stairs. They were surprisingly not slippery. Whatever that magic stuff was, they must use it here, she thought.

She walked to planters on the railing and felt around for the spare key. Only, there wasn't one. She checked all the planters, sure that was where Felicia had told her to look.

Nothing.

Unsure what to do next, she walked to the front door and heard a soft snuffling sound.

"Hey, Webster," she called.

The puppy yipped excitedly.

Noelle reached for the door handle and found it turned easily. She pushed it open.

Two things happened at once. A very excited fifty-pound German shepherd puppy bounded out toward her and she saw a duffel bag in the foyer.

Noelle automatically patted the enthusiastic dog. He licked her hands and wiggled before dashing down the stairs and heading for the trees on the side to take care of business.

"It's slippery," she called after him, only to realize he had magical feet because he returned at the same hyperspeed with which he'd left and never skidded once.

"Good boy," she said, hugging him.

Problem one solved, she thought. Which only left the mysterious duffel and the open front door.

The bag could be Carter's, she thought, picturing Gideon's thirteen-year-old son. Or it could be the proof that some evildoer had broken into the house and was, even as she stood there, ransacking the place. Either way, she had to find out.

She stepped cautiously inside, the eager dog at her side. By the front door was an umbrella

stand. She grabbed the biggest, most threatening umbrella she saw and held it in her hands like a club. She was tough, she told herself. After all, she'd taken a self-defense class earlier that fall. Of course, her instructor had warned them all against walking *toward* trouble.

"If you're in here to steal stuff, I've called the police and I'm heavily armed," she yelled as she walked through the open area of the main floor. There was a big living room and a huge kitchen. She knew there were bedrooms at each end of the house and more living space downstairs.

Webster enjoyed the game, staying at her side, his wagging tail thumping against the wall at regular intervals.

"Just walk out with your hands up and no one will get hurt," she continued.

She paused, listening. There was a sound from the hallway. She turned, umbrella poised. If necessary, she would hit the guy, then run. She was pretty sure Webster would run with her, thinking this was just more happy puppy fun.

The bathroom door opened and a guy stepped out. A tall guy wearing nothing but jeans. He had a towel in one hand and was using it to rub his just-washed hair. In fact, staring at the tall, well-muscled man, Noelle would guess he'd just washed the rest of himself, too.

She paused in the middle of the hallway as several thoughts moved through her brain. First, few burglars bothered to shower while on the job. She didn't have actual working knowledge of that as fact, but was willing to assume it was true. Second, while she knew she'd never seen the man before, something about him was familiar. Third, he was really handsome, with light brown hair and dark blue eyes. And had she already mentioned the body to her brain? Because it was good, too.

They stared at each other and she remembered her list. *Right. Fourth...* Her gaze dropped and she swallowed. He had a nasty-looking cut on his left hand, complete with raw flesh, black thread from stitches and—

"Oh, no," she whispered as the edges of her consciousness seemed to fold in on herself. "Not blood. Anything but blood."

For someone who had been through what she had, it was pretty funny that the sight of blood made her woozy, but there it was. Life with a sense of humor. Her stomach roiled, her skin got clammy and she knew she was about an eighth of a second from crumpling to her knees. If that happened, she didn't think Webster was up to saving her.

She bent down to shorten the distance to the floor and hopefully save herself from a lasting brain injury.

GABRIEL BOYLAN STARED at the half-collapsed blonde. "This is why I hate the suburbs," he told her as he dropped his towel and moved toward her.

"Can you hear me?" he asked, speaking loudly.

She waved toward his hand. "Keep that away from me."

Her voice was weak and she seemed to be swaying. He swore under his breath, noticing even as she started to go down that she was still brandishing that ridiculous umbrella in his direction. *Great.* His brother had fallen for someone insane.

He grabbed the umbrella and twisted it out of her grip, then lowered her the rest of the way to the floor. She groaned. He took in her paleness and rapid breathing and figured she was close to fainting.

The annoyed, I-really-don't-like-people side of him wanted to let it happen. At least unconscious she would be less trouble. But the doctor in him knew that wasn't the right decision. He shifted her so she was on her knees, then pushed her head down.

"Head lower than the heart," he told her. "Slow your breathing. You're fine."

"You can't know that," she managed to say.

"Want to bet?"

When it seemed like she was going to stay conscious, he returned to the bathroom and quickly

wrapped his left hand. The deep cut was still tender and oozing. He was lucky—he'd been stupid to get injured in the first place, but while it was ugly, no permanent damage had been done. A good thing considering he needed his hands to make a living.

When the tape was secure, he shrugged into a clean, long-sleeved T-shirt, then walked back into the hallway.

The woman had straightened and was staring up at him. Her gaze dropped to his hand, then darted away.

"Thank you for covering up," she said, her voice low.

He assumed she meant the wound and not his chest. "You're welcome."

The puppy settled next to her, leaning heavily on her, ready for the next round of whatever it was they were playing.

"You're sensitive to blood," Gabriel said.

The woman winced. "I know. It's ridiculous. I always have been. You'd think I would get over it, but no. Oddly, I can deal with getting a shot, as long as there's no bleeding. Otherwise, I have to close my eyes." She drew in a breath, then looked at him. "Who are you?"

Gabriel frowned. "Gideon didn't tell you?"

"I haven't talked to him recently." She paused, as if trying to remember how long it had been. "I

guess I've seen him in town but we haven't spoken."

Now Gabriel was confused. "You're not Felicia?"

The woman scrambled to her feet. She was a tall blonde—too skinny for his taste, but pretty enough. She wore black jeans and a ridiculous sweater decorated with tiny Santa heads. As he'd said before—the suburbs sucked.

"No, I'm Noelle," she said. "Who are you?"

"Gabriel."

He was going to say more but her blue eyes widened. "Gideon's brother?"

He nodded, unable to figure out why someone he'd never heard of was chasing people with an umbrella in his brother's house. Not that there was an appropriate place for that sort of thing.

She smiled. Whatever else he was going to grumble about faded as her mouth curved. Because the second she smiled, he felt a whole lot better about nearly everything. His hand hurt less, he wasn't as tired and the avalanche of regret he felt at showing up in Fool's Gold reduced itself to a small rockslide.

Talk about a trick.

The smile widened. "Oh, wow. I didn't know you were coming for sure. You're the doctor, right? Felicia mentioned she'd asked you to stay for the holidays, but I thought you'd said you couldn't

make it. I'm Noelle Perkins. Felicia and I are friends. I have a store in town and I know Gideon, of course. And Carter."

The son his brother hadn't known he had, Gabriel thought. There was a situation.

"Gideon and Carter are shopping in Sacramento. Felicia got stuck in town and asked me to come and let Webster out." Her smile faded. "Oh, no. I attacked you. I'm really sorry."

"It's okay," he told her. Mostly because it was and partially because he wanted to see the smile again.

"I couldn't figure out why the door was open and the spare key wasn't where she'd said."

"Gideon told me about the key, too, and I used it."

"Of course."

The smile returned and his breathing relaxed.

She bent down and collected the umbrella. "I took a self-defense course a few weeks ago. Just a Saturday afternoon of basic stuff. My instructor would so kill me if she knew what I'd done, so if you could not say anything I'd appreciate it."

"Not a problem."

She glanced quickly at the bandage, then away. "Um, what happened to your palm?"

"I was an idiot."

"It happens to all of us."

"I should know better."

She flashed the smile again. "And the rest of us shouldn't?"

"Fair point," he told her.

She waved the umbrella. "I'll put this back." She started down the hall. "Do you want some coffee?"

"Sure."

She went into the kitchen and pulled out mugs and two small pods filled with coffee as if she knew her way around the place.

He was still having trouble wrapping his mind around the fact that his brother was engaged and had a son. Not that the two events were related. Carter's mother had died a couple of years ago. As for Felicia… Gabriel frowned as he realized he didn't know how she and his brother had met. The fact that he hadn't spoken to anyone in his family in over a year might have something to do with that.

Webster followed Noelle and looked hopeful as she collected spoons and started the coffeemaker. She eyed him.

"I'm pretty sure you've already been fed," she told the dog.

He wagged his tail.

She sighed. "You're so demanding. Fine. I'll give you a cookie."

Webster woofed at the word and followed her to the pantry, where a plastic container of bone-shaped treats sat on a shelf.

"But just one," she told him, waiting until he sat to give it to him.

He took it gently and bolted from the room.

Gabriel watched him go. "He's not much of a guard dog. He let me in without a growl."

"He's a puppy," Noelle said. "Felicia wants him to be friendly rather than aggressive. He's supposed to be Carter's dog, but she's the one who takes care of him. He's been to a few obedience classes but they don't seem to be taking."

She motioned to the large table and he moved forward to take a seat. Noelle added the first pod and pushed the button, making sure the mug was positioned underneath.

She leaned against the counter. "So, you're here for the holidays. To be with your family. That's nice."

"I haven't seen them in a while," he admitted, trying to remember the last time he'd joined his parents and brother for Christmas. *More than a decade,* he thought. *Fifteen years? Longer than that?* Maybe it had been before he'd left for college. "Feel free to fill me in on what I've missed."

"I've never met your parents," she said cheerfully. "I know Gideon, of course. He moved here before me. It was last year. I just got here in the spring." She wrinkled her nose. "It was before the whole snow thing. I'm going to have to take some lessons or something. It's a lot more slippery than I

realized. I know there's an ice element, but I didn't think it was, you know...*ice*." She made air quotes as she spoke the last word.

He chuckled. "You have a lot to look forward to."

"You mean aside from warmer weather?" She turned back to the coffeemaker and pulled out the mug. "How do you like it?" she asked, already moving to the refrigerator.

"Black is fine."

"That's such a guy thing."

She pulled out a container of flavored coffee creamer, then handed him his mug and returned to the counter. She obviously knew her way around the kitchen. Because of Felicia, he told himself. Women who were friends hung out a lot doing stuff like having coffee. He supposed it wasn't that different from going out and having a drink.

She stuck in a second pod, put a mug in place and hit the button.

"You know Gideon bought a couple of radio stations," she said.

He nodded.

"He does an oldies show every night. Lots of songs I've never heard of but most of them are good. Felicia runs the festivals in town. She's very organized. Carter's in school, of course." She glanced at Webster, who sat with his tail wagging. "What about you, young man? Any career plans?"

The puppy barked.

"Impressive." She glanced up at Gabriel. "Sorry. I talk to everything."

"It happens."

She got her own coffee and poured in the flavored creamer, then set the container back in the refrigerator. She took a seat across from him and tilted her head.

"What else can I tell you?" she asked. "I have guilt about trying to attack you."

"With an umbrella."

She laughed. "I'm not sure if that makes it better or worse."

He liked how amusement danced in her blue eyes and the flash of teeth when she smiled. He wanted to keep her talking because the sound of her voice soothed him. A ridiculous claim, but there it was. What he couldn't figure out was why. *Why her?* He was around women all the time. Other doctors, some of the nurses and techs, soldiers, administrators. But Noelle was different somehow.

"How long has Carter been around?" he asked.

"He showed up this past summer. His mom died about a year before that. He was in foster care with his best friend's family. They'd made arrangements with Carter's mom before her death, I think. But they started having marital trouble and he was going to have to go into the system. He didn't have

much to go on—his dad's name and that he'd been in the military. But he found him and made his way here. I don't think I could have been that resourceful at his age."

"Me, either," Gabriel admitted.

He cupped the mug with his good hand. The wound on his left palm throbbed in time with his heartbeat. If he were his own patient, he would tell himself to take something. That being in pain didn't reduce the time to heal. But he also knew he wouldn't listen. That he didn't want the mental wooziness that was a side effect and that he was a long way from the threshold of what was unbearable.

"You know they're getting married, right?" she asked. "Gideon and Felicia."

"I'd heard."

"There aren't details yet. At least not that I know of, but I can't see them waiting." She paused and raised her mug. "I should probably warn you about her."

"Felicia?"

Noelle nodded. "She's really smart. However smart you're thinking, you're not even close. She's beyond genius level, although I don't know what that's called. And she speaks her mind, which I adore, but it can surprise some people. She just flat out says what she thinks. So you don't have to be

subtle around her. Oh, and she's super beautiful. If we weren't friends, I'd have to hate her."

The last statement was delivered cheerfully.

"You're good at speaking your mind, too," he said.

She shook her head. "Not really. I try to be honest. You know, not waste everyone's time with game-playing. But it's a tough habit to break. I'm not advocating being mean at all. That's not right, either. But I think the world would be a better place if we all stuck a little closer to the truth."

She paused and the corners of her mouth turned up. "I have no idea where *that* sermon came from." She stood. "I should get back to my store before I start boring you with my theories on the meaning of life."

"You have theories?" he asked as he rose.

"A few, but trust me, you don't want to hear them. Anyway, I also need to get back to my store because in an effort to save money I hired part-time college students instead of full-time regular people."

"College students aren't regular people?"

"Not usually. And especially not when there's a dusting of fresh powder up on the mountain. I live in fear of returning to my store and finding the door propped open and no one inside. Well, no one who works for me." She paused. "It's weird because the high school kids I've hired are really responsible. So I guess at nineteen they regress."

He had no idea what she was talking about but that was okay. Just listening to her voice was soothing. He also appreciated the information about his family. A case could be made that he should have known it all himself, but he didn't.

"It was nice to meet you," she told him. "And I am sorry about the umbrella."

He waved off the apology. "You okay to get down the mountain?" he asked.

She blinked at him, then her eyes widened. "Crap and double crap. My car's stuck in a snow-drift."

Crap was her idea of a swear word? She wouldn't have lasted in Kandahar an hour, he thought, amused.

"I don't suppose you know anything about winter driving?" she asked.

"As a matter of fact, I do. I went to medical school at Northwestern and I've been stationed in Germany more than once."

"Whew. Good. Then maybe you wouldn't mind backing my car out of the drift? Then I can sort of point it down the mountain and I'll be fine."

Instead of answering, Gabriel walked to the front door. Despite being barefoot, he headed out onto the porch and saw her small import nose-first in a bank.

There were skid marks on the driveway and a

couple of places where it looked as if she'd fallen on her way up to the house.

"This really is your first winter," he said.

She moved beside him and sniffed. "I have other talents."

He was sure that was true and he wanted to tell her they were likely far more interesting than an ability to drive in the snow. But she was a friend of his future sister-in-law and this was a small town and he wouldn't be around for very long. All good reasons to only say, "I have no doubt."

He stepped back into the house and waited until she'd joined him to close the door.

"Give me a second to put on boots and I'll drive you back to town."

"You don't have to go to that much trouble."

"Someone has to. I doubt you can make it on your own. Pointing the car in the general direction of town is not an option."

NOELLE NODDED AT the nice, handsome doctor before he turned away and retreated to the guest room. She sighed, thinking it just wasn't fair. He was single—at least she thought he was—and she was single. She wasn't sure what else they had in common, but there had to be something. Regardless, she obviously hadn't impressed him in the least.

Oh, well. There were worse fates, she told her-

self. Just as soon as her busy season was over, she was going to get into a relationship. Maybe she would join one of those online dating services, or see if there were clubs for singles in town. If nothing else, she could put the word out with her friends. Most of them had recently fallen madly in love.

Maybe there was something in the water, she thought as Gabriel walked toward her, taller now in sensible-looking snow boots.

"Keys," he said as he approached.

She dutifully held them out. "I'm sure once I'm out of the snowbank I'll be fine."

"I doubt that," he said, shrugging into his jacket. "You'll be a menace until you hit flat ground."

"That's not very flattering."

He looked at her, his blue gaze steady. "Isn't it true?"

"Sure it is, but you're being kind of blunt about it."

"I thought you liked blunt."

"Not as much as I thought."

She made sure Webster was secure in the house before closing the door and following Gabriel to her car. He told her to wait while he backed the car out of the snow, which he did in one easy move. The tires didn't even skid—something she considered a personal betrayal. When she got her car

back in the garage, they were going to have a little one-on-one conversation.

Gabriel stopped beside her and opened the passenger door. She climbed in, instantly struck by how close the seats were and how much broader his shoulders were than hers. She fastened her seat belt and as she did, she glanced at him.

He had a nice face, she decided. A little guarded and there were shadows under his eyes, no doubt from his hand injury and maybe traveling. But he was someone she would instinctively trust. Not that her instincts were anything to brag about, she thought. Look what had happened with Jeremy.

Or not, she thought, facing front.

"Is that the way?" he asked, motioning with his left hand.

Instantly she felt herself getting woozy. "Be careful with that," she murmured. "It's like a weapon."

He glanced at the bandage. "There's hardly any blood."

She leaned back and closed her eyes. "Just the *b* word itself is bad. Yes, go down this road about three or four miles. At the bend in the road, turn right. Follow the signs and you'll be heading into town."

She pressed a hand to her stomach and told herself to think pure thoughts. Or at the very least, distract herself.

"You picked a really good time to visit," she said, knowing she was about to babble, and not caring. Babbling was better than fainting. Or throwing up. "There are always festivals in Fool's Gold, but more so during the holidays. There are a couple of parades and a live nativity. I can't wait for that because there's going to be an elephant."

"In a nativity?"

"Don't judge. You don't know for sure there wasn't an elephant at the birth of baby Jesus."

"I'm actually pretty confident there wasn't."

"Priscilla is a part of a lot of celebrations in town. She's a member of the community, too."

"Priscilla the elephant?"

"Do you know any other Priscillas?" She risked opening her eyes and was pleased to see that there was no bloody bandage in her peripheral vision.

"She would be the only one."

"Okay, turn there," she said, pointing when they reached the bend. "Follow that road into town. You'll turn right on Frank Lane."

"Who's Frank?"

"I have no idea. It's by 4th, which is where my store is. But yeah, Frank. I guess there's more town history I have to learn."

"You know about the elephant. That should count."

He was nice, she thought, wondering if there was a subtle way to ask him to coffee. Or dinner.

She glanced at his large hands resting on the steering wheel and wondered how badly things would go if she mentioned a sleepover.

She pointed to her store and he pulled in front and parked the car.

She turned to him, prepared to offer a heartfelt thank-you, only to realize there was a problem. "How are you going to get back to Gideon's house?"

"I thought I'd go find Felicia."

She risked a quick glance at his hand, then turned away before she got faint. "Are you up to it?"

"I'll be fine. Just point me in the right direction."

She looked into his eyes and smiled. "I thought you didn't believe in that."

"My concerns were specifically about your driving."

"I want to take offense at that, but there's the whole snowbank issue that makes it less valid."

They got out of the car and she gave him directions to Felicia's office. He handed over her car keys.

"Thanks for the ride back," she said, wishing she was better at the boy-girl thing. She used to be relatively okay at it. Obviously the lack of practice was showing. "I hope we run into each other again.

Not literally," she added, glancing at the snow still lodged in her fender.

"I'd like that," he said.

She returned her attention to him, trying to judge what he was thinking. But his dark blue eyes gave nothing away. He smiled and gave a wave, then turned and started in the direction she'd told him.

Noelle watched him go. When he turned the corner, she hurried toward her store, only to come to a stop when she saw the sign on the door.

Gone skiing. Come back later.

New York Times **Bestselling Author**

SUSAN MALLERY

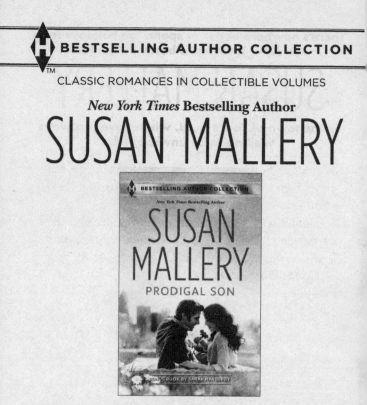

George Hanson's oldest son, Jack, was pursuing his dream of becoming a judge—until his father's death called him home to try to keep the family business afloat. Samantha Edwards is a creative dynamo at the company, but she and Jack butt heads over office issues. Can beauty and the boss set their differences aside to devise a plan to save the business—and plan a wedding, too?

PRODIGAL SON

Available December 31, wherever books are sold!

**Plus, enjoy the bonus story *The Best Laid Plans*
by Sarah Mayberry, included in this 2-in-1 volume!**